Matlock the Hare

Also by Phil and Jacqui Lovesey

The Riddle of Trefflepugga Path
The Puzzle of the Tillian Wand
The Trial of the Majickal Elders
Upon a Tzorkly Moon

SilverWood

Published in 2018 by SilverWood Books

SilverWood Books Ltd
14 Small Street, Bristol, BS1 1DE, United Kingdom
www.silverwoodbooks.co.uk

ISBN 978-1-78132-746-3

British Library Cataloguing in Publication Data
A CIP catalogue record for this book is available from the British Library

Page design and typesetting by SilverWood Books
Printed on responsibly sourced paper

The League of Lid-Curving Witchery

Acknowlededgments

It would be both unseemly and 'untzorkly' not to acknowledge the kindly folk who helped make this slender volume the majickal-wonder it now is. Both the author and illustrator send their humble and heartfelt thanks to all those who brave and generous souls who made the impossible happen, in particular the following:

Cork; Hazel Lambert, Barry Moth & Bertie; Henry, Maude & Heathcliffe; Katie Henthorn; Trevor A. Ramirez: Linda A Boone; Leigh D. Lyle; Charlotte Ruddick; Marie Stephenson; Frances; Cathy Brown & John Grisswell; David Watson Mackenzie; Deborah S. McCormick; Caroline T. Swope; Edie Evans; Professor Stephen Candy; Emely Pul & Aaron Zsoldos; Vanessa J. Farbrother; S.J. Medcalf; Isabella Macy; Amy Pouse; Katherine Hazelton; Lynn Hoagland; Ravensfire; Toni Drew Wulff; Kevin Wigley; Paul. A. Withers @pawprintwildlife; Jackie Lovesey; Peter & Jax Lovesey; Anne Watson; Spiritunicorn; Louise Whiddett & George Page; Stephen Booth; Val Thurlow; Emma Gregory; Claire Tolliday: Ian McFarlin.

Advice before Reading…

Although the following book has been fully endorsed by *The League of Lid-Curving Witchery*, they are witches, and frankly their motives for doing so might not be so transparently well intentioned. Hence, a few precautions were felt necessary by the author and illustrator to ensure maximum reading pleasure whilst ensuring minimum exposure to any accidental, unforeseen or unpleasant side effects.

Therefore, the following guidelines have been issued to readers:

NEVER attempt to say, speak or chant any of the spells out loud, as doing so could result in any number of 'splurked' behaviours or unsightly physical symptoms.

ON NO ACCOUNT attempt to copy any recipes, unless you are already in receipt of an official *League of Lid-Curving Witchery* cauldron and stirring utensils.

The domestic broom (or besom) shouldn't EVER be used to attempt flight. Any such occurrence could well involve permanent injury and/or prolonged humiliation.

DO NOT attempt to read the book backwards – as it really won't make any sense, and besides any secret-messages from the witches are hidden a lot more cunningly than that!

PLEASE do not lend this book to anyone of a frail disposition.

The suggested ideal reading- environment is somewhere safe, relaxed and with a mug of brottle-leaf brew, or a large glass of Grimwagel wine close at hand.

Introduction

by Ursula Brifthaven Stoltz Grand Tzorkly
High-Priestess of 'The League of Lid-Curving Witchery'.

Welcome, good readers of these 'griffles' – or 'words' as you would know them. As current Tzorkly High Priestess, one of my many duties is to further knowledge of our league to all creatures. Indeed, as I travel the Majickal Dales in my role as ambassador for the creature-sisterhood, one of the questions I'm most frequently asked is 'How did it all start?' And the truth is that after you've answered it for the 100th time to a group of clottabussed leaning-jutters, the whole 'ambassador' business gets rather tiresome and exceedingly splurked.

So it was with this in mind that I decided to let the chroniclers of Matlock the Hare's adventures tell the story for me. After all, they did a reasonable job of making Matlock appear far more heroic than he is in real life in his trilogy (I know this for a fact – believe me, he's a complete splurk!) Initially they were somewhat reluctant, claiming their previous experiences with creature-witches had proved most unsettling. However, after a few stinging vrooshers from my wand, both seemed more than ready to accept the honour of telling the League of Lid-Curving Witchery's story.

The result is the book you now hold in your hands (or paws) – an attempt to reveal the true beginnings of our tzorkly-sisterhood via the legends of three of our most prominent witches: Algorin, Veyanor and Sinchkin. I hope it will give you much-needed insight into the ancient, majickal origins of our 'world' – one league that unites and respects the cultural divisions of the many covens and solitary-witches that now comprise it.

I also hope it means I don't have to keep repeating the same stories over and over again, as those who know me from Matlock's adventures will appreciate my patience can wear rather thin at times.

Enjoy the journey with my ancient forebears – and always 'rise above'!

Yours, in eternal tzorkliness,
Ursula Brifthaven Stoltz

Parlawitch – Some Essentials…

During the following pages you may well encounter a word or two that leave you adjusting your witches' hat and scratching your head. Chances are, it's from Parlawitch, the early-adopted language of all creature-witches that can be traced right back to small island clusters off the Norwegian coast.

What follows is a short glossary to acquaint you with some of the basic words and expressions before departing into the darker recesses of this book…

Groydelshlammen! – (n) Curse delivered when something has gone *splurked*.

Gerrshlohm – traditional Parlawitch greeting from one tzorkly-witch to another.

Gruhmlauffen – (adj) applied to anything that might be miserable – *ie 'I met a jick-beetle with only one wing this today, t'was most gruhmlauffen'*

Moon-turn – (n) Twenty-eight days. The time it takes for a complete 'turn' of the moon.

Oidy – (adj) Small. Occasionally also used as *'peffa-oidy'* – meaning 'very small'.

Saztaculous – (adj) Something that is really majickal, memorable and splendid.

Sazpent – (n) A dragon – derived from *'a most saztaculous serpent'*.

Splurk – (insult) Something (or *someone*) that is incomprehensibly dim or stupid. Can refer to a situation, decision, or simply another witch you know to be several ladles short of the full cauldron.

Spuddle – (n) A cross between a legend, myth and most majickal piece of folklore.

Stroff – To kill, be killed, perish, or die. Altogether something to probably be avoided.

Twizzly – (adj) – Scary – something (or someone!) that might give you a case of 'the twizzles'.

Tzorkly – (v/adj) – 'to rise above', the creed of the craft. The ability to ascend from all that may be harmful or distracting – the ultimate aim of any witch.

Vroosher – A majickal-bolt fired from a wand. Often blue in colour, the tip of the wand will *'frizz'* first before the vroosher is unleashed. Although *vrooshers* can cause majickal illusion and other strange effects, most are simply shot from the wand to maim or kill (*stroff*).

The Ancients, Howling Lands and The Spuddle of Algorin

To begin at the beginning is to know it's also an end; mere chance born from the circumstance of any number of unrelated moments and middles...

The shadowy world of the creature-witch is as far removed from that of human-witchery as it is from the small Nordic islands where they once lived. Whilst certain similarities are obvious; hats, brooms, robes, wands, cauldrons, covens and spells – here it pays to look into history. It was creature-witches who *first* adopted these now familiar trappings, human witches subsequently appropriating them afterwards. Indeed, without the creature-witches, many of the things most associated with witchcraft might never have seen the light of a dark and treacherous day. For instance, it was the smaller, furrier creature-witches who first made and wore pointed hats (the conical design serving two functions: varying lengths and patterns signalling different covens, whilst the wide brim provided protection from driving winds and rain). It was creature-witches who first fashioned round cauldrons, spotted the potential for flight by broom, soon mastering the skill to rule the skies. More or less everything we associate with 'our' witches is taken from the creatures. But who were they – and more importantly, what was their story?

This much we do know...

Creature-witches first appeared some 1400 years ago in small covens on the many islands in and around Scandinavia. To this day, their language of Parlawitch still contains many Nordic influences, affirming their ancient roots to this cold, unforgiving region. Whilst many details remain as elusive and frustrating as the witches themselves, early traces of these strange creatures can still be found in ancient Norse poems telling of epic Viking journeys in storm-tossed seas, when a fearful crew of raiders sailed too close to dark rocky outcrops they knew as 'The Howling Lands'.

Temur, warrior chief of the Raumarici,
Took to Icy Seas, and –
daring its currents swept,
To pass his men by The Howling Lands,
Where Odin's foul sisters raged and wept.
Their screams would rip the strongest sail,

And in the air they flew on sticks,
And Temur knew his men would fail,
If lured ashore by such deadly tricks.

It's not known how many Viking longboats were wrecked by such 'deadly-tricks', but the Vikings held a healthy respect for the 'foul sisters'. Some experts even suggest the warlike figureheads on their longboats were originally carved to frighten creature-witches away and give safe passage between the islands. Whatever the truth of the matter – it seems marauding Vikings quickly learned to literally steer well clear of the much smaller witches. A wise precaution.

Today, the same small islands are no longer home to the creature-witches, their fortunes changed by the unwelcome arrival of a cruel and unforgiving winter that would be forever remembered for its unrelenting harshness, pushing the witches to the very brink of survival, testing their majickal prowess and dividing them with bitter discord. During such times, one creature-witch was to stand-tall and rise above the others to become one of the most legendary figures at the centre of league mythology – Algorin, the famed warrior-witch who led her black-hatted sisters across The Icy Seas to forge new beginnings in faraway lands.

Algorin

The Spuddle of Algorin

Fourteen hundred years ago, amidst a cruel and dark winter, a line of robed figures in pointed hats make their way slowly across a snow-covered beach towards a captured Viking longboat a short way out in the chopping, grey surf. Waves swell and break under the heavy sky as sheeting rain slakes the shore, stinging the creatures' faces. Some stumble and have to be helped. Others stand further back on the shoreline, watching their fellow-sisters slowly unfurl the large sail, the wind instantly tearing at the bindings, turning the boat for the seas beyond. Both parties begin to chant. Offerings are left on the shore to wish the voyagers luck, while those on the longboat can only look back as their homelands recede, wondering if they'll ever return again.

The Great Crossing had finally begun…

The Howling Lands

It was the winter that would only ever be remembered by the lucky few that Algorin chose for the journey – the small band of creature-witches and familiars that set sail with her. The others would starve and perish, their bodies frozen in deep snows that would cover the islands for many months to come. Most likely knew their fate the moment the longboat left the windswept shore. In that one bleak instant an era ended, those about to perish watching the chosen few embark on a journey that would one day establish the beginnings of *The League of Lid-Curving Witchery.*

But such thoughts were far from Algorin's mind as she stood in the prow of the ship, freezing winds tossing her long red hair. Instead, her mind raced with the dangers of the journey ahead. What great beasts would they encounter in these unforgiving seas? Would the majickal-lands her mother spoke of really exist? And if so, what waited for them there? All Algorin had were her warrior's instincts, a deft blend of savagery and cunning that had built her fearsome reputation in *The Howling Lands* – a name that she herself could take sole credit for; for hers were the howls that had lured others to their grisly demise…

Born to Ragnhilda, a solitary creature-witch, Algorin had soon learned her mother's skills for survival. Not belonging to any coven, the life of a solitary witch was one of constant vigilance. With food in short supply, the covens hunted as voracious packs. Any living creature was seen as food – including solitary witches. Often, covens would battle amongst themselves, uneasy truces frequently broken as they searched for ever more precious resources in the barren, rocky islands. Great battles raged in the skies, dozens of witches taking to their brooms and vrooshing each other in the hope of stroffing as many as possible. Some survived many such battles, while others fell horribly to their deaths, witches on the ground squabbling for the felled flesh, furs, robes, brooms, hats and wands. Hard times called for desperate measures.

In between such deadly rivalry, solitary witches eked out an unseen existence. To be found risked a terrifying fate at many cruel hands. Often taken to one of the many large caves inhabited by the covens, there the unfortunate solitary witch would be boiled alive in a large cauldron until the meat fell from her bones, as the others jostled for a bowl of the dreadful soup that remained. Algorin knew every awful moment of the Solitary Ritual, having witnessed her own mother's death when she was captured by the infamous Long Claws, the most feared coven on the islands.

Watching in the darkness a short distance from the cave, its mouth glowing from the flickering fire of the bubbling cauldron, her young eyes never left the awful spectacle, every scream seared into her memory as she swore terrible vengeance on them all...

A full five years passed before, under a clear and cloudless night, Algorin walked into The Long Claws cavern and slaughtered each and every one, not stopping until she ripped the final claw from their dead paws, storing them in a leather bag around her waist. The spuddle of Algorin the Fearless had begun.

Word quickly spread amongst the other covens. All now dreaded a similar visit from the flame-haired solitary witch. And come she did, visiting each in turn, not a trace of fear in her eyes, easily dodging any vrooshers fired her way. But this time, she came with gifts she'd taken from the Long Claws: the hats, brooms, robes and wands of the dead. Fear soon turned to relief as each coven collected their spoils, overjoyed Algorin hadn't exacted her wrath on them.

So it was that a hunted, solitary creature-witch became accepted into the previously forbidden world of coven-witchery, able to move between all islands upon whatever whim possessed her, whatever bidding she desired. Algorin was both feared and revered. Occasionally, a foolish coven-leader unwisely pitted her champion against her, only to be savagely vrooshed and stroffed, either on land, or in the air. For Algorin was exceptional at both, her mother having taught her well. Algorin could strike faster and more accurately with a wand than any other witch on the islands. On a broom, she could out-manoeuvre any

rival at breakneck speeds. And whilst some coven-witches knew the true reason for Algorin's vengeful glare, few ever dared to speak aloud the fate that befell her mother. Those that did died with the words on their lips.

None knew of the majickal world far from the Howling Lands. This secret, given to her by her mother, remained with Algorin alone. At times, she would sit on a rocky outcrop, staring out to sea, recalling her mother's words when she'd once taken her to the highest cliff and pointed far over The Icy Seas.

"These lands," she'd told her, "are nothing compared to what lies beyond. True, they are our home, but only because none has ever sought to seek another, or look beyond these splurked horizons. But there are other lands, full of so many different and majickal things – and you will be the one who finds them. The moon will be your guide, for they cannot be reached by broom alone. Everything I have taught you will come to this."

Algorin watched her mother scatter rune-stones at their feet, reading them by the light of her wand in the still, silvered night. "It is foretold. You will make the journey without me. Come, there is much to do to prepare you for the twizzliness that lies ahead. Your time will be upon you all too soon."

And so it proved, as Algorin's mother was captured by the Long Claws soon after she had finished teaching her daughter all she knew. As she was led towards the horribly bubbling cauldron by the jeering coven, Ragnhilda simply smiled, knowing that if anyone would cross The Icy Seas, it would be her beloved daughter.

But first, there was the small matter of The Deadliest Winter – and a boat...

Winter Witches

With its unrelenting climate, creature-witches wisely learnt to respect the long winter that often ravaged The Howling Lands. Thick furs were worn in multiple layers and only the most necessary hunting trips were undertaken, the witches travelling in groups, armed with heavy zweidel-hammers to break the ever thickening ice their wands couldn't crack. When hunts failed, the weakest familiar would be sacrificed as food for rest of the coven, skinned and cooked in the large cauldron that hung in the centre of the cave.

Wood for the fire was a constant priority, unfortunate familiars sent out into the icy-depths to constantly forage for whatever they could find to keep the cauldron blazing at all times. Fish was dried above it, seaweed draped on its vast rim, and high above hung a small bowl of warming oestbalm oil, essential to keep wands working to vroosh away hungry predators that got too close to the luring safety of the cavern during the unforgiving, endless nights.

Of all the winters the creature-witches had endured, The Deadliest Winter was by far the harshest. It swept in late one September like a vengeful dragon breathing pure ice and freezing everything in its path. Trees fell apart, their heavy limbs cracking and dropping to ground already frozen hard as stone. Life on the small islands was decimated. The only hope was to try and survive around a fire in one of the caves, hoping it wouldn't be occupied by a coven of hungry creature-witches.

As the winter deepened, Algorin knew the time had come to discover if the majickal-lands were anything more than an ancient spuddle. But how? No broom could ever fly that far. The witches were stuck, freezing and starving to death. Whatever spells and majick they possessed proved no match for the unending cold.

But one day, for just a brief spell, the winds died and snows stopped. Algorin left her shelter and headed through the frozen woodland to the high cliffs overlooking The Icy Seas. At the edge, she stopped, eyes narrowing, her curiosity drawn by something quite unexpected – a great sea-dragon, its one wing unfurled above a vast body floating on the chopping waves. A menacing head sat on a short neck, the wide body flowing away to reveal a series of wooden legs appearing to walk over the water. It was like nothing she'd ever seen before, yet she knew was a sign, and most importantly, one that had come from somewhere truly majickal and far beyond all that she could see – from over the distant horizon itself.

Throughout that short winter's day she excitedly tracked the dragon on her broom as it rounded each island. She began to wonder if it was lost and needed luring in. Occasionally, her ears and nose would twitch as the sea breeze bought strange new sounds and smells. Sometimes, she thought she heard chanting, as if many voices were calling out across the swell. Other times, she picked up peculiar scents unlike any she'd smelled before. Certainly, this strange dragon needed closer inspection, and taking to the skies, wand drawn, Algorin flew out and boldly circled above the vast creature.

Which was when her heart leapt...

The 'dragon' was a vessel – a huge boat, its 'wing' catching the wind to guide it. The 'legs' were moved by other, smaller creatures with hard heads and horns, chanting as they went about their work. This was the moment she had been waiting for, the way she'd fulfil her destiny! The longship would be hers – and with it, the prize of leaving these wretched islands once and for all...

By nightfall, she had a plan and recruits from the covens to help her. They flew by broom, some settling on the beach to light fires, others flying out to sea, Algorin at the front, urging them on, drawing her wand against the wind and letting fly with the first vroosher, watching its blue bolt streak harmlessy into the waves a short distance from the Viking ship. She hadn't missed, but instead struck precisely where she'd intended. The plan wasn't to destroy the vessel, but to drive it onshore where her black-hatted sisters eagerly waited to deal with the peculiar creatures on board.

Circling above, other witches let fly with their wands, vrooshers screaming like comet tales into the pitch black sea, the noise and fury so loud that those few who survived would forever know these islands as The Howling Lands from that night onwards.

Panicking, the Vikings took to their oars, others desperately sending arrows up onto the night to down the fearsome flying beasts. Some simply jumped overboard, terrified at the spectacle. In all their many voyages, none had witnessed anything like it. Odin's foul-sisters had surely risen from Valhalla to take vengeance for wickedness on their part.

Above, Algorin watched the chaos, calling the others away when the boat began to turn towards what it assumed was the safety of the shore. However, one witch hadn't heard, and in her enthusiasm made one final, plunging dive, wand drawn. An arrow struck her. Hurtling towards the sea, she let one last vroosher fly, the lethal blue bolt striking the large sail and setting it ablaze before she crashed into the churning waters.

From The Howling Lands, they flew on sticks
Where Odin's foul sisters raged and wept:
Screams and wands that ripped and tore,
And sent the burning dead to the shore

Algorin knew her dream of escaping the islands was burning up before her widening eyes. As the flames turned the dark seas orange she swooped down, landed on the blazing deck and vrooshed the last of the terrified Vikings, before signalling the witches waiting on shore to wade out and grab the hull. Behind, others on brooms vrooshed the waters, creating swell to push the longship to the shallows before it finally beached on the pebbled shore just as the burning mast crashed into the breaking waves.

They'd done it. Against all odds, the creature-witches had captured a Viking longship – a deed that would be forever remembered in Norse folklore. Those Vikings that managed to make land in less hostile territories would forever tell of 'Odin's foul sisters' that 'flew on sticks', whilst warning of the dangers of venturing too close to The Howling Lands.

On shore, Algorin watched the witches set about the spoils. There were chests full of exotic treasures and thick sealskins. Bodies were soon looted of weapons, shields, helmets and furs before being tossed into fires. Flagons of mead and wine were eagerly seized, the witches squabbling for the choicest cuts of dried fish and drink.

All the while, Algorin planned. Whatever lay beyond the dark horizon, it wouldn't be these witches she'd take with her. Weary of their savagery, she saw no sense in taking such creatures to new and majickal lands. She watched as yet another dead Viking was tossed into the flames, a shower of bright red sparks spilling up into the night. Not for Algorin the spoils from the boat. For her, it was the vessel itself, the chance it offered to leave the misery of her island life. But who to take with her? She needed others a different kind of witch; reliable and trustworthy. But how to find them? Algorin couldn't decide, watching with a heavy heart as the soaking body of the drowned witch was pulled from the waves and hurled into the flames to a chorus of drunken cheers.

The Howling Lands had no place for sentiment. But looking at the longship, Algorin knew the great vessel was her only hope to one day finding it in new and faraway lands...

The Choosing

By next morning word had spread of Algorin's great deed, the many island covens flying to the beach to stare in awe at the 'twizzly seadragon'. The chaos of roaring brooms quickly roused other witches sleeping on the wet sand. Fearing a raid on their newly acquired plunder, many drew their wands to defend their valuable treasures and furs.

Sensing trouble, Algorin sent a booming vroosher high into the sky, its terrifying noise silencing all where they stood. And what a moment it was. Frozen in an ominous tableau of wide-eyed greed and aggression, it was the first time every coven-witch had ever met in one place. The dangers were horribly obvious.

All heads turned to Algorin, waiting to see what she'd say.

She smiled, almost savouring the moment, with half a mind to simply leave and let them settle it by wands amongst themselves. Certainly, most would probably perish – but those that remained would undoubtedly be the most vicious and untrustworthy. Less than ideal seafaring companions.

Instead, she walked to the boat and climbed aboard, standing by the charred figurehead, wand drawn above her head. "Sisters!" she cried. "This dragon came to these shores from faraway lands. It brings supplies; furs, food and drink to help us through this splurked winter. But still the weakest amongst us won't survive. Our majick is no match for the moon-turns ahead. Therefore, I declare that some will venture with me upon the seas for different shores, new lands hidden beyond the horizon."

A gust swept the beach, witches shivering as biting cold tore through their furs.

"Preparations need to be made!" she continued. "A giant wing is needed to catch the wind. Food has to be foraged for the journey ahead. And there will be a choosing of those that I will take over The Icy Seas alongside me. Therefore, in one moon-turn's time, a contest will be held.

Those who prove themselves worthy will journey with me."

Algorin's mother had not only reared a great warrior-witch, but a cunning one, too, and Algorin's plans for a contest were far from what the creature-witches might have expected. Thirsting for the chance to prove themselves the best flyers, wand-wielders and spell-casters, each coven busily set about choosing its champion to represent their honour, practising their skills despite the icy weather. As such, their efforts were to be largely in vain.

In the days leading up to the choosing, Algorin travelled between the island covens, watching preparations for the contest. However, instead of assessing the champions, her warrior's eye sought out those witches and familiars who looked most disinterested, or who busied themselves with more essential tasks like gathering food and wood for the fire. Those creature-witches so keen to impress with their fighting skills were instantly dismissed from Algorin's mind – although she did nothing to quell their enthusiasm for the contest.

A full month passed, and the covens assembled back on the beach where the Viking wreck lay. Firstly, Algorin commanded the best flyers to set off on their brooms and return with the tallest, straightest tree they could find. When they did so, she scornfully mocked their efforts.

"You were charged with returning with the tallest, straightest tree, you splurks!" she said, kicking the pile of trees on the sand. "That meant just *one* tree between you – not one tree each!"

The cold, exhausted witches looked to each other, knowing that none could ever work with the other.

Algorin turned to another group lurking towards the back of the crowd. "You there – trying to hide! Take to the lid, return with the longest, straightest tree!"

A short while later, as the crowd huddled on the windswept shore, the small group returned, flying an enormous tree-trunk between them; a triumph of skill, balance, strength and practicality. Algorin smiled as she addressed the successful witches. "I watched you when I came to your covens. None of you pay heed to individual glory, instead working quietly for the benefit of your sisters. Such loyalty will now be rewarded. Together, you have passed my flying-task and shall be the first to travel with me."

The crowd began to mutter, the better flyers seething that they hadn't been selected. Algorin sensed the mood turning and quickly issued the next task, brandishing a broken oar from the longship and pointing to the smaller trees still lying on the sand. "Those must be made into oars. They must be smooth, strong and ready for the twizzliest seas."

The remaining witches set about the task with savage and furious determination, squabbling to seize a tree and blast the freezing bark away with their wands, and vrooshing any others who dared get close. Just as before, Algorin quietly selected another group at the back of the crowd and set them to the same task on the larger tree. "This will be the main mast," she quietly told them. "Make it sturdy and straight to survive the harshest storm."

They did so, working together in the surrounding chaos, using their familiars to clear away stroffed bark and branches as they smoothed the clean trunk with their wands, then carried it into the longship and lashed it upright.

"It'll need a wing," one told Algorin, "to catch the wind."

"Indeed, it will," she agreed. "What is your name?"

The witch frowned slightly. "Utharde. Why?"

"Because, Utharde, you and your fellow sisters will make such a wing and travel alongside me to the majickal-lands."

"And if we have no desire to do so?"

"You have no desire to live somewhere new?" Algorin pointed at the beach where the others still squabbled and fought over broken trees. "You desire to spend the last of your moon-turns freezing and stroffing with sisters such as these?"

Utharde thought, watching snow-clouds gathering ominously on the darkening horizon. "We'll need food, familiars, furs and more luck than has ever been granted to any witch, ever."

Algorin fixed her in the eye. "All we need, Utharde, is to believe."

Burr
Dop
Froo
Frass
THE HOWLING LANDS
The Great Crossing
THE MAJICKAL DALES

The Great Crossing

It was a day that was as foul, freezing and unforgiving as any that Odin could conjure when Algorin and her chosen crew finally set sail. The remaining witches looked to their spoils from the wrecked longship in the doomed hope of somehow surviving the coming months. Those too weak to fight over the precious seal-skins, weapons and food had already perished in large numbers, their bodies forgotten in deep snows covering the islands.

Despite the conditions, Algorin's crew of chosen witches and their familiars had worked hard to restore the longboat, closely examining its workings, using the abandoned Viking tools to make it seaworthy once more. Utharde oversaw the making of the great sail, organising familiars to prepare pelts and sew it together. Others worked on carving a new figurehead. The old dragon's head was torn down, its place taken by a figure just as fearsome – Ragnhilda, Algorin's own mother, her arm outstretched, wand pointing resolutely towards some distant horizon.

"You see, mother," Algorin quietly whispered as the new figurehead was fixed into place, "you will be coming with me, after all."

On the day they set sail, other surviving witches gathered on the snowy shore, chanting as the crew made their way out to the longship where Algorin and Utharde already waited, helping them aboard as the cold, grey waters lapped around the thick wooden hull.

"Don't be twizzled, sisters," Algorin encouraged. "Our new beginning has arrived. A majickal destiny waits for us beyond the edge of The Icy Seas."

Those that felt less assured said nothing, fearful of what lay ahead, yet all too glad to be leaving the ravages of the hostile winter. Silently, they took their places behind the oars, instructing their familiars to do the same.

"Whatever lies ahead, whatever splurked beasts the sea sends, we will

prevail!" Algorin cried, sending one last booming vroosher high into the heavy grey sky, the explosion echoing round the bay. "It is time, sisters! Time to find the lands beyond the horizon. Do not show fear, do not be twizzled. Remember, those that also once made this great ship came from such lands. And just as they too crossed The Icy Seas – then so shall we!"

She nodded to Utharde, who unleashed the heavy sail, the boat immediately lurching as it billowed and caught the wind.

"Don't worry," Utharde assured Algorin. "It will hold."

Algorin looked at the straining cloth, a large witch's hat emblazoned in the centre. "It's not the wing that twizzles me," she quietly murmured, gripping her wand as the longboat slowly swung out to sea. "It's what we have no knowledge of yet, but will come to know all too soon."

Yet for all her fine words, courage, belief and determination to find new lands, Algorin knew nothing of the sea and its mysterious tidal workings. She simply knew it was vast and most likely unending. Just how unending, she had no idea, just as she had no idea if its depths, or what unknown creatures may lurk deep in the inky black. Many times she had flown high above its glistening surface only to return without ever glimpsing a distant line of land on the horizon. But now, as her homelands disappeared, she realised first-hand the sheer scale of the unforgiving emptiness of it all. It was so much bigger than she could ever have imagined, so much more twizzly. She glanced towards the stern, seeing Utharde already braced against the large rudder-oar and instructing witches to secure the sail in order to try and cut through the swell and steer the straightest possible course.

"Which way?" Utharde shouted above the roar of the wind.

Algorin slowly turned to her mother's figurehead. "Show me, Mahpa," she whispered, watching the outstretched arm pointing the wooden wand towards the horizon, and willing it to move.

A large wave crashed into the side of the hull, sending freezing water tumbling inside. The impact was so great it slowly turned the boat sideways, boat and figurehead now pointing in another direction entirely.

"This way!" Algorin cried. "Follow the wand! She will guide us there!"

And whatever the others may have thought, all knew it would be fatal to question Algorin. The winds grew and seas steadily became wilder, but

on the boat there was just a fearful silence, everyone aware that by simply following the wand they were now heading into a looming storm.

One witch had a suggestion, grabbing her boom. "I could take to the lid. See if land lies ahead, then return."

"Who else thinks this is a good idea?" Algorin asked as the waves surged once more.

No one raised their aching, clawed hands.

Algorin turned to the witch, her smile as icy as the sea. "Then go. Find our new lands. Tell us which way they lie. Go."

The witch needed no further encouragement, quickly straddling her broom and soaring away into the darkening sky.

"You think she'll return?" Utharde asked her.

Algorin shrugged, calmly taking out her wand and shooting a bright blue streaking vroosher into the clouds. Moments later, both witch and broom fell to the sea. "I rather doubt it." She turned to the others, fire in her eyes. "Who else wishes to leave? Who else wants to fly back home? If you do, do so now! I dare you. Take your chances against me and my wand!"

Not a single witch or familiar hardly dared breathe.

Satisfied, she put away her wand as a huge lightening bolt crashed overhead, flashing the seas white and shaking the boat. Utharde quickly ordered oars shipped and the sail broken down and fixed like a canopy above their cowering heads. "We must shelter! Now!"

For the next few hours, the witches and their familiars huddled under the sail as the storm raged all around them. Great waves tossed the boat, spilling into the hull, the witches frantically scooping icy water into their hats and throwing it back overboard as quickly as they could.

"Can't we use our majick?" one desperately asked, brandishing her wand.

Another massive thunderclap exploded overhead. "You think a wand could stop this?" Algorin laughed. "We go where the storm takes us and trust it has our destiny in its heart."

"But we could all stroff!"

"Trust me sister, another sound from you and you'll be the next one that does."

Algorin looked into the fearful faces of her crew, knowing their uneasy disquiet would soon give way to mutiny. The very fact that she'd managed to get this far was nothing short of a miracle in itself. But expecting further loyalty through threats and promises wouldn't last. The longer the storm raged, the more she felt black eyes turning on her. She had to do something to quell any rebellion.

"Sisters," she told them. "This storm has been sent to guide us. We must be full of strong hearts. We must have the courage to hoist this sail once more. For while we cower like twizzled beasts underneath it, we go nowhere. Now is the time to ride the storm and discover where it truly wishes to take us!"

Utharde joined her as they watched the great heavy sail being slowly hauled back up, the wind instantly stretching every stitch as it was lashed to the violently rocking hull. "This is splurked, Algorin! We shall all stroff!"

Algorin smiled. "I would rather stroff as a warrior of The Icy Seas than hide in a stolen boat. What about you?"

Utharde held her stare for as long as she dared before making her way back to the stern and seizing hold of the long rudder. "Hold fast, my sisters! We've conquered the air on our brooms – now let's ride the seas on this dragon!"

The great boat turned in the raging wave as the roaring wind surged it forwards, witches and familiars clinging to each other and whatever they could find. At her mother's figurehead, Algorin drew her wand and defiantly sent out a vroosher into the heart of the storm, driving rain and seawater lashing her face. "Take us, Mahpa! Take us to the majickal lands!"

For three more terrifying hours the ship was left to the mercy of the elements, until at last the rain began to ease, sea calmed and black clouds slid away to reveal a sky alive with a thousands glittering stars. It was as if the storm hadn't ever happened, had simply been a nightmare they'd all shared and now woken from.

"It's beautiful," Algorin gasped.

Utharde nodded, the ship now thankfully quite still, barely a breath of wind in the sail, the sea a near-perfect mirror of the wondrous night sky above. She pointed to the largest group of stars, tracing the outline with her long fingers. "Idla," she muttered. "She shows herself to us for our courage."

"Idla?"

"The Soothwing," Utharde replied. "Messenger from the stars, sent by the Ancients to guide us."

Algorin stared at the constellation, gradually making out bright points of a great bird with outstretched wings and an unmistakeable pointed hat on its head. "Why is she here?"

"Why don't you ask her?" Utharde smiled. "It's what your mahpa would have done."

Algorin frowned, watching Utharde take out a handful of small pebbles from a bag around her waist, recognising them instantly. Each was adorned with its own carved symbol. "How did you get those?" she demanded. "They belonged to my mahpa."

"Indeed. You're mahpa's raven stones. Ragnhilda gave them to me, for this moment, to give to you. I trust you can remember how she taught you to throw them?"

Algorin hesitantly took the stones, feeling their familiar weight, before scattering them on the floor of the boat and trying to make sense of the pattern. It was pointless. To her they were simply stones, whatever meaning they may have contained was quite beyond her. "I cannot read the symbols. She never taught me."

"Because it was never you that was meant to read them," Utharde calmly replied, before pointing up at an enormous full moon beginning to slowly rise from the distant horizon.

"What is this majick?" Algorin hissed, reaching for her wand. "Why did you have my mother's stones? Who are you, really?"

Utharde simply smiled, quite unconcerned. "I am a solitary creature-witch, as your mahpa was, also. You have no reason to fear or mistrust me. After all, it was you who freely chose me to travel alongside you. No one forced your hand, mind or wand to make such a choice. And just as your mahpa's destiny and mine was once forever entwined, so mine is now entwined with yours. Your choice made it so, Algorin." She pointed to the scattered stones. " And these raven stones will reveal the true majick of that destiny. Look to the twinkling-lid, Algorin. See who comes from the Ancients themselves to read them."

Algorin looked, eyes narrowed, slowly making out a large black bird flying in front of quite the brightest yellow moon, as if it had almost emerged from within it. She gasped, watching as it gracefully dropped to sweep low over the stilled sea, wings outstretched, a witches' hat clearly visible on its black head. "Idla?"

"The very same," Utharde confirmed, the bird angling and spreading its open wings to rise up and land on the side of the boat, its eyes glinting in the moonlight as it glanced down and carefully studied the scattered stones, head to one side, to a series of low caws and clicks issuing from its throat.

"How does it know what they say?" Algorin whispered. "It is just a bird. It cannot speak or tell me such things."

"Hush," Utharde replied, reaching out an arm then gently lifting the strange creature right up onto Algorin's shoulder. "Close your eyes, sister. You'll soon hear her words."

Algorin did so, feeling the long beak nuzzling her wet hair, then suddenly gasping as a majickal explosion of light seemed to catch her entire body. It was if nothing else mattered in this one majickal moment.

"Now Idla is ready to show you," Utharde said, watching Algorin's eyes dance and flicker behind her eyelids. "Listen with your heart."

Gradually, Algorin began to hear a distant voice; calm, gentle, yet somehow resonating with the wisdom of all the black-hatted ages:

Through the majickal veil,
After the eight legs have been,
You will rise above,
To tzorkly lands I have seen.
There to begin your true destiny,
Far from these twizzly Icy Seas.

"What does she say?" Utharde asked, the others on the boat silently watching the strange ritual. "What did the stones tell her?"

Algorin slowly opened her eyes, looking into the piercing blackness of the soothwing's face. "That we will rise above. That we will find new and majickal lands. That they will be tzorkly."

"Tzorkly?"

Algorin watched as the bird flew slowly back out into the moonlight. "I have no idea of what it means, either."

Utharde took a breath. "Your mahpa once talked of this word to me."

Algorin narrowed her eyes. However much she liked Utharde, there was too much about her she didn't understand. She picked the rune stones up from the wooden deck, questions needing to be answered. "How did you have these?" she asked accusingly. "Why would my mahpa give them to you? Why haven't I ever met you before? Just who are you, really?"

If she was at all twizzled, Utharde didn't show it, her voice as calm and steady as the boat upon the sea. "The stones were always mine. I gave them to Ragnhilda a long time before you were even a glint in her witch's eye."

Before Algorin could say any more, something else had begun to make her hackles rise. All around the boat, a series of bubbles had slowly crept from the depths and now broke on the calm, glassy sea. Witches and familiars peered overboard, equally confused.

"Wands at the ready, sisters!" she commanded, as something began urgently scraping against the underside of the hull. "Whatever lay below has been woken by the storm." She gripped the end of her wand, its tip already frizzing bright blue.

"What is it?" a panicked witch cried. "What's down there?"

"I'm not so sure," Algorin replied, the surface beginning to ripple and thrash, "that it's one of anything."

All around the boat, long, brittle legs broke the water. Bulbous, scarred, barnacled abdomens followed.

"Sea-spiders!" Utharde cried, seeing horrifying fangs and sets of glowing red eyes. "Stroff them, sisters, or we drown here!"

The others needed no further encouragement, letting fly with streaking blue vrooshers as dozens more of the beasts surfaced, each as big as the creature-witches themselves, hooking their long front legs onto the hull and hauling their heavy bodies up onto the boat. Three familiars were quickly taken, dragged and tossed into the sea. More spiders climbed the sides, the blue vrooshers merely bouncing off their hard bodies.

"Our wands are splurked!" Utharde cried, watching three spiders quickly surround one witch and drag her screaming into the sea.

Algorin instinctively reached into the small bag around her waist and pulled out one of her stolen long claws. Its tip was still razor sharp. "Use these!" she cried, throwing it at the nearest spider as it reared, watching it tear into the soft green underside, the great beast crying out and crashing to the deck, its legs thrashing madly. "Take them!" she ordered, handing claws to as many witches and familiars as possible. "Stroff the eight-legged!"

The witches hurled the claws as the sea-spiders reared, quickly throwing the twitching bodies overboard. Other spiders began climbing the sail to escape, their long sharp legs ripping into it, the whole ship rocking and swaying perilously.

"The mast!" Utharde cried. "It's breaking!"

The wood began to crack under the weight, before snapping and slowly falling into the sea, spilling spiders back into the icy waters as others pulled the huge mast down into the depths until nothing remained by the merest trace of receding bubbles.

For a while, the only sound was the short, sharp breaths of those on board, the sea once again as calm as it had been before the attack.

"They'll be back," Algorin quietly said. "This time for the rest of the boat."

"What did Idla say to you?" Utharde pressed.

"That the eight legs would come. And after, a majick veil that we will rise above. I have no idea what it meant."

"Yet it must be true. She's the voice of our ancestors, the soothwing of the lid."

They busied themselves trying to heal the wounded, cutting away dangling ropes and repairing leaks in the battered hull. By dawn's first light Algorin was able to see the damage the sea-spiders had wrought. She counted the blank and weary faces. A third of their number were gone. They were tired, hungry – and worse – aimlessly floating in a calm sea. With no mast, they had little choice but to row, but for that they'd need food. A fire bowl was lit under a small cauldron, the witches filling it with seawater and sacrificing an unfortunate familiar and boiling it into soup.

Algorin watched the other familiars huddling at the far end of the boat, fear on their faces. Some, she knew, would soon jump overboard and take their chances in the sea rather than be eaten. And with no sign of land, how long could the witches survive? She accepted a bowl of the horrible broth, chewing on the stringy meat. Was this where it all ended? What of the majickal veil? How would they 'rise above' and find these 'tzorkly' new lands Idla had spoken of? And frankly, why believe a splurked crow, anyway? Algorin believed in the real, the natural, the now. The majick of stones and prophecies were no match for the wand and broom. And yet, the very reason they were all facing death in a bro-ken boat, lost in the middle of The Icy Seas, was surely down to no one other than herself, and her simple desire to prove her mother's prophecy right. But as to how many more would perish, she had no idea.

"The others are nearly at an end with this," Utharde said, joining Algorin with a steaming bowl of stew. "Another night like the last and they'll turn on us – then each other."

Algorin softly laughed. "The eight-legs will stroff us all first. I have no more claws, our wands are useless and our ship is splurked. We can row, but where to?"

Utharde turned to the figurehead. "Your mahpa still points the way."

Algorin sighed. "My mahpa, Utharde, stroffed many moon-turns ago." She pointed to the boiling cauldron. "In just the same way as that poor familiar did. It's why I took my revenge."

Utharde smiled. "And also why you had the claws, Algorin. Almost as if this moment was foreseen, and your mother knew why you would need them one day. Ragnhilda was a fine and great witch, Algorin. A seer, I believe. Who's to say she didn't know exactly why she did the things she did?"

Algorin frowned. "I don't believe in such things."

"It isn't your place to believe. It's your place to get us to the majickal-lands. We must be ready for the veil and what comes within it."

Algorin watched Utharde return to the others round the cauldron. For while she looked at the discarded raven stones by her feet, before, with a sudden roar of outrage that startled the boat, she threw them as far as she could into the freezing waters and angrily turned to her mother's figurehead.

"Show me!" she demanded. "Show me the way! I'm lost, mahpa, and whatever you thought I was, wherever you thought my destiny was, it has come to nothing! Your stones are as splurked as your words! We will all stroff because of you!"

And then, as the others watched wide-eyed, the figurehead slowly began to crack and turn, its wooden eyes opening fiery red, the wand sweeping round to point back inside the boat.

"It's alive!" a familiar gasped, scrambling to hide behind retreating witches.

But Algorin held up her arm, refusing to be cowed, staring into the red eyes, her face set. "Show us the way, mahpa."

The figurehead slowly cracked and moved again, its wand now pointing back out to sea into columns of thick white fog rising from the very places where each stone had landed. The majickal veil had arrived.

"To oars!" Algorin commanded, the boat slowly moving as witches and their familiars started to heave together. "Row, sisters! My mahpa, the great Ragnhilda, shows us the way!"

The witches hauled as hard as they could, pulling on the oars until their lungs burned and they were left exhausted and drifting in the choking fog.

Algorin fetched her broom, Urtharde trying to stop her. "It's too splurked to fly! You'll never find your way back."

Algorin brushed her aside. "As you said, it's my place to get us to the majickal lands."

She watched as Algorin soared into the white, the sound of her roaring broom quickly smothered in the thickening veil. She turned to the others. "Ready your wands! We need to let off booming vrooshers to guide her back!"

An elderly witch, struggling behind her oar, managed to splutter, "Let her go. Let her be lost. She's the splurk that's bought us all to our deaths, anyway."

Utharde calmly whispered in her ear. "Sister, your words betray your anger, not your ambition. I'd make them your last, if you want to utter any more."

The witch reluctantly drew her wand, waiting with the others for Utharde's signal before firing it up into the fog, the sky exploding in thunderous blue.

Far above, barely hearing the distant booms, Algorin flew on, diving as low as she dared to find the edges of the fog. Twice, she almost crashed into the sea, only veering away at the last as it suddenly rose up, eager to snatch and drown her. No matter how high she soared, the fog remained, never thinning, seemingly unending. She was hopelessly lost, the faint booming vrooshers now lost to her ears. Her long red hair began to freeze as her claws slowly lost their grip on the icy broom handle. She knew the end wouldn't be long. Soon, she would fall into the sea. She wondered what it would be like to drown, drifting ever deeper into the unforgiving black. The splurked soothwing had told her to 'rise above' so she'd taken to her broom and done exactly that. But in the end she'd failed, a destiny unfulfilled, a ridiculous ambition that had cost too many lives for nothing. Readying herself for what was to be, she closed her eyes and pointed her broom down towards the sea…

…landing with a painful jolt a few moments later on a terrified huddle of witches and familiars right back on the deck of the boat.

"Groydelshammen!" she exclaimed, painfully hauling herself to her feet as the others moaned and groaned. "What are you doing here?"

Utharde gave her back her hat. "The lid is curved," she said, looking up into the fog. "It bought you back to us. It's where you belong."

"The lid is curved?"

"There is no other explanation. However far you'd flown, you would have always ended up here. The lid must be majicked. Curved."

Algorin looked at the miserable faces; some shocked, some twizzly, some completely blank. In all her years she'd never seen such a dispirited bunch of witches. The journey and the long preparations had broken them. Or perhaps she had broken them, with empty promises and a dream of a destiny that was never really hers to either live or tell.

Taking a breath, she turned to them. "Sisters, what I see before me is no coven I would ever want to be the smallest part of. Because what I see is more than any coven. It's more than me, more than you, more than any of all our ancestors that went before us. What I see is a league. A league of black-hatted sisters who had the courage to strike out and venture for new lands. A league who battled the storm, the eight-legs and this lid-curving veil." She fixed them all. "I see what we will ever be known as – I see The League of Lid-Curving Witchery!"

She drew her wand, aiming it high up into the fog. "And I, as your leader, thank each and every one of you that joined me. For this journey will become legend, sisters. You will become legend. From this sun-turn forth, we and all our descendants will forever be known as The League of Lid-Curving Witchery, and there's not one of them that won't wish with all their black-hatted hearts that they weren't here with us right now to make this journey!"

Her wand started to frizz. "Draw and loose your wands! Not as a coven, but as a league for the very first time – The League of Lid-Curving Witchery!"

Roused, the witches stood, aiming their wands and shooting bright blue vrooshers into the fog, as deafening explosions echoed all round.

"Again!" Algorin cried. "The veil is lifting!"

Vroosher after vroosher shot up from the boat, volley upon volley, the fog thinning with each burst. Even cowed familiars cheered in delight.

Soon, it was over, the fog lifted. But The Icy Seas hadn't finished with them. The breathless witches watched in stunned silence as the

bright morning sun seemed to suddenly shoot in an arc across the sky and plunge the day straight back into night.

A witch hissed at Algorin, fear in her eyes. "What majick is this that can bring back the night?"

Algorin looked to the horizon, slowly beginning to smile. "The majick of our new home," she replied; pointing to a thin back line in the distance. "Land, sisters! I see land!"

The others looked out, excitedly jabbering and pointing.

"To oars!" she ordered. "There lies our home!"

Witches and familiars once again set to, hauling the boat through the chopping swell, cheering each stroke despite their exhaustion. Utharde steered at the back, concern spreading over her face.

"What's wrong?" Algorin called over.

"The boat is turning! I can't stop it! It's going its own way!"

Alglorin looked towards the land, an awful panic rising. It had quite gone! She ordered everyone to stop rowing, keenly scouring the horizon for any signs.

Utharde joined her. "It's splurked. We've just been rowing in circles."

"Groydelshammen!" Algorin cursed, following the swaying wooden wand of her mother's figurehead, willing it to settle and point in one direction. "Show me, Mahpa," she whispered. "We've come so far. Don't let it end here."

Slowly, the arm began to move, the heavy wet wood creaking, the wand inching up into the clear night sky. Algorin followed its aim, seeing an ominous dark shape circling above and a vivid burst of orange flame against the moon.

"Dragon!" she cried, as witches immediately readied their wands. "And it's ganticus!"

A young witch, keen to impress, grabbed her broom and set off into the night.

"She'll stroff!" Utharde cried, watching the dragon twist in the air then plunge towards the lone figure.

"No," Algorin replied, admiring the young witch for her courage and skill in the air. "She's leading it to us. Ready the ropes!"

The witch dived and flew just above the boat. Although fast, she was no match for the enormous beast, who let out a powerful jet of flame, scorching her robes.

"On the next pass, throw the ropes!" Algorin ordered. "Nobody vroosh! We need this dragon, sisters, more than any of you know!"

The brave witch turned, this time diving even lower, Algorin guiding her closer, the huge dragon roaring as it gained, the sea churning with the wind of its vast wings.

"Now!" Algorin yelled.

A dozen ropes were hurled to the witch, who caught one and expertly looped it around the twisting tail. The dragon roared, turned its head, but didn't let out more flame, no matter how easily it could have apparently stroffed the little witch.

It was a magnificent moment, the importance of which didn't escape Algorin. "To brooms!" she ordered. "You know what to do! Lash the beast!"

Other witches quickly took to the sky as their familiars hauled ropes from the sea to fling them back out and as high as they could, the boat beginning to dangerously spin in the foaming water as the dragon slowly became lashed, its enormous clawed feet and paws harnessed by the many witches circling all around it.

Utharde watched from underneath. "Why does it not stroff us? It could do so with just one breath!"

"Because," Algorin grinned, gripping tightly onto the sides as the whole boat was suddenly lifted out of the water, "we are 'rising above', Utharde! We are being 'tzorkly'!" She started to laugh as the boat rose high into the sky, the dragon's huge wings slowly flying them gracefully through the sky in quite the strangest airborne caravan; dragon, boat and triumphant outriding witches cheering on their brooms. "It's the majickal moment, Utharde. The moment The League of Lid-Curving Witchery finally became tzorkly!"

Utharde smiled, looking up in awe at the magnificent beast above them.

"Land!" one of the outriding witches suddenly cried, pointing with her wand. "I see it, Algorin!"

Algorin looked to the welcoming landmass moving closer with each re-affirming flap of the dragon's wings. Relief flooded over her. Was it really possible, or just another trick of the seas?

"It is taking us to the majickal lands!" Utharde laughed.

"No," Algorin replied. "*She* is taking us home. Our new home."

"She?"

"Of course," Algorin frowned. "You think a male creature could ever be this tzorkly?"

Utharde leant against the side of the boat, holding her hand out to the breeze, feeling it flow through her open claws. Everything, finally, felt *right*, a destiny foretold now happening, a new beginning rising from The Icy Seas after their long and perilous journey. Briefly, she thought of the others they'd left behind in The Howling Lands; friends she'd known that would now be facing the worst of all winters. She turned to Algorin, who seemed to have read her thoughts.

"They were never chosen, Utharde. Whatever the runes have in store for them was never part of our destiny."

"You believe in the raven stones now?" Utharde asked. "The same witch who cursed and threw them into the sea?"

Algorin said nothing, noticing a single stone still lying on the deck etched with a star pattern on its surface. Somehow she'd missed it when she'd thrown the others, yet now recognised it immediately, hearing her mother's words when she'd explained its meaning: *The star, Algorin, signifier of the great 'now' that has been deemed the moment for reaching your dreams'*. She looked beyond the dragon into the night sky. It had never seemed more beautiful, or more majickal. A sense of peace engulfed her, yet with it also a creeping unease. What if the majickal lands weren't quite so majickal, after all? What really lay in store for them there? What creatures lived in such a place where great dragons freely flew out to sea? How many would there be? What powers would they have? Would they welcome a weary band of creature-witches, or simply stroff them on sight? Just what had she really bought her fellow sisters to?

She watched the joyous witches and familiars eagerly pointing at the rapidly approaching horizon, trying, but unable to fully share their joy.

Utharde joined her. "There are splurked times ahead?"

Algorin half-smiled. "There are always splurked times somewhere. We just have to hope ours are less so."

Utharde nodded, looking back over the side of the boat as

a sudden shaft of sunlight broke from the horizon, the dragon letting out a deafening roar as it fell across its face.

"She greets the new dawn," Algorin observed, watching the land below gradually light up in a sweeping series of pink and golden flashes. "I think it's time for us to greet our new home."

Witches and familiars watched the unfolding scene below. The lands were vast, so much bigger than anything they'd ever known, stretching interminably in all directions, the sea now a distant memory, reduced to a thin blue, glittering line in the far distance. The dragon seemed to know exactly where it was taking them as it followed a wide river upstream, a golden ribbon bordered by high mountains, forests and lush green meadows.

"Have you ever seen such beauty?" Utharde gasped. She felt the sun on her face, basking in its warmth. "What foods cannot fail to grow here?" She grabbed Algorin by the shoulders. "Everything is plentiful. No more will we starve, or have to search for firewood. Truly, Algorin, your mahpa was right – it *is* majickal!"

Above the dragon slowed, its huge wings billowing back to hold the air as it hovered and slowly descended.

"It's lowering us!" a witch cried.

"Be ready to cut the ropes," Algorin ordered, watching the ground rise up and trying to judge the moment. Above, the dragon appeared to be concentrating just as hard, its huge head checking the descent on either side of the boat. "Now!"

The witches vrooshed the ropes with their wands, the large hull bumping the last few inches onto the soft earth. The great dragon let out one final fiery blast before it turned and headed back up into the morning sky. In moments, it was just a small flying dot silhouetted against the sun.

For a while, there was simply silence, as witches and familiars cautiously helped one another onto the lush, mossy ground. Circling witches on their brooms landed, they too in quiet awe of their new surroundings. They were on the edges of thick woodland by a large open flatland in the bottom of a steep-sided valley. A river gurgled through the middle, the only noticeable noise in the vast landscape.

Algorin scanned the mountainsides, then set her eyes to the woods, shafts of sunlight dropping into the gloom like plunging swords.

"Are we alone?" Utharde quietly asked.

Algorin shook her head, instincts on highest alert. "No. Whatever it is, whoever they are, they're watching."

"Are you sure? I see nothing."

Algorin withdrew her wand and sent a screaming blue vroosher into the trees sending a group of startled birds into the sky. Further back, other creatures could be heard calling to one another with peculiar, strange new cries echoing deep in the gloom.

"We must stroff them," a nearby witch urged, readying her wand.

"No," Algorin replied. "If they meant to harm us, they would have done so by now." She addressed the others. "Sisters and familiars of *The League of Lid-Curving Witchery*, we have travelled far to find these lands. But they are not our lands. They belong to those that watch us. We do not know their strength, or numbers. If they come too close, vroosh above their heads and below their feet. Do not hit them. Show no fear, instead mercy. None must stroff, for we do not know what allies we will need in such a ganticus new home."

"But if we stroff some, the others will leave us alone," the witch insisted.

Algorin bent down and whispered in her ear. "Sister, have you come all this way, only to stroff over some splurked words?"

The witch swallowed hard. "No."

"Because if *anyone* stroffs today – then so too will you."

"I'll vroosh above their heads and below their feet," the witch muttered.

"Good," Algorin replied, lightly tapping her hat with her wand. "It would be such a shame to stroff you. But I would, you know that, don't you?"

The witch nodded, admonished.

Next, she turned to the familiars, pointing into the woods. "Take axes. Bring four of the straightest, strongest trees." She instructed a group of witches to go with them, before turning to the rest. "Dig four holes, one for each post." She pointed to the boat. "Empty it of everything. We will turn it over. It will be the roof of our new home –

the first great hall of *The League of Lid-Curving Witchery*."

Everyone set to, the sound of axes in the forest mixing with digging. The great cauldron was set on the ground, then four posts set into the deep holes around it. Familiars hooked ropes and slowly hauled the heavy hull from the ground, gently turning and setting it in place on the four posts.

As Algorin issued the orders, she also watched the edge of the woods and steep mountain sides. Occasionally, she glimpsed strange creatures. Some had horns, others looked three times her size. Some were clothed, others simply had fur. But all silently watched every move the witches made.

"When will they come for us?" Utharde asked when she returned with familiars loaded with firewood. "I hear them in the woods. At night, is that when they'll stroff us?"

"Tend to the walls," Algorin instructed. "They must be built before sundown." She looked over at the half-completed hall, the wooden wand on the inverted figurehead now pointing down over the entrance as if guarding their new home. "My mahpa will keep us safe."

That night, as familiars returned with foraged food, the tired witches gratefully feasted around the huge cauldron in in their new hall. Algorin deliberately left the heavy doors open for any interested eyes to freely see inside. Several cautiously approached, lured by the orange glow, briefly peering in at the strange new visitors before hurriedly scurrying away.

"They're twizzled by us," Utharde observed. "They know the majick in our wands."

Algorin nodded. "They must understand we will only take what we need from their land and no more. There will be peace, if they are peaceful, too."

"But others will soon hear about us. They might not be so peaceful."

Algorin said nothing, lost in her thoughts as she watched the flames dance under the heavy cauldron. She had achieved her destiny, journeyed and found majickal lands. Yet deep in her witch's heart, she also knew that really, what ended with her was merely the beginning for so many others. She had done all she could, and would rule for as long as time would allow. But as for the future? She smiled briefly to herself. Would she have thrown the raven stones one more time if she still had them? Would she *really* want to know what lay in store? Instead, she walked to the open doorway to where her mother's figurehead now looked to the stars, her wand pointing at the ground.

"As above, so below," she quietly said, climbing up onto the roof and staring at the stars far above her head.

In the woods beyond, small eyes glowed in the darkness. How long would such a delicate peace last? What splurked creatures would one day emerge to investigate further? What would become of, and how would history ever remember, the once-humble origins of *The League Of Lid Curving Witchery?*

Many years later, as Algorin took her final breath, much had inevitably changed. And in the generations that followed her death, changed further still. The once tiny encampment by the river had grown spectacularly, the great hall of the original travellers abandoned and largely forgotten as a thriving trading town grew up all around it. Over time, just as Algorin had suspected, creatures of all kinds had arrived, easily outnumbering the witches, claiming the land for themselves and calling it Trasgar.

Yet perhaps most importantly, no blood had been spilt in its slow occupation, no lives lost. During Algorin's rule, witches wands had never been vrooshed in anger. Following her passing, Trasgar grew once more, creatures of all kinds arriving in this most beautiful and plentiful of all places, before settling and building homes, the surviving witches quite unable to stop them. How could they? The land belonged to the creatures in the first place – the witches were merely visitors. But as such, they were tolerated, mostly seen as strange objects of mild amuse- ment. Some creatures had heard how the witches had once supposedly crossed The Icy Seas in the same rotten boat that now stood abandoned on pillars in the centre of the village, but quickly dismissed it as simply 'a clottabussed old spuddle, not even worthy of the telling'.

The spirit, the fight, the pride of *The League of Lid-Curving Witchery* had all but vanished. It would take another special witch to make them tzorkly once again...

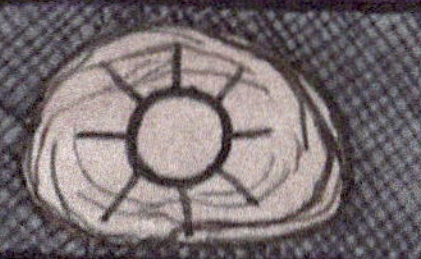

As Above

So Below

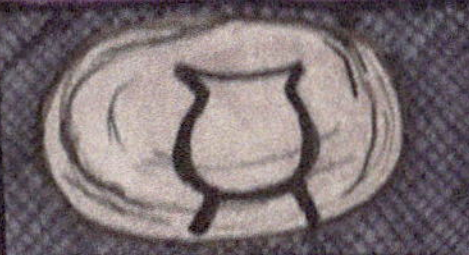

Trasgar, Treachery
and The Spuddle of Veyanor

In the four centuries since Algorin passed to the Ancients, much had changed in the small settlement she eventually managed to find and call 'home'. And really, this was all she *ever* called it, seeing no reason to give it any other name. 'Home' sufficed, and felt right. For beings that had spent most of their lives moving from one cavern to the next in The Howling Lands, this lush new land represented a permanency, the chance to finally settle. Food was plentiful, the climate agreeable and with so few of them, the likelihood of fatal squabbles greatly reduced. Gradually, they'd all learned to trust one another, bound by their perilous journey across The Icy Seas, and forever in Algorin's debt for getting them there.

So how had so much changed? What had happened to turn such a special, majickal and quiet place into the bustling medieval town of Trasgar, with its hundreds of houses, market, shops and traders? A town where those remaining witches were side-lined into their own 'quarter', vastly outnumbered by all manner of strange and peculiar creatures they could have never imagined drawing a single breath, let alone so casually overrunning their precious and hard-won 'home'.

The answer lay in the unfortunate collision of trade with Algorin's determination for peace at all costs. Just as she and Utharde had suspected, their new homelands were far from uninhabited. On their very first night they had cautious new visitors scrittling around outside, sniffing and searching, their voices low, hurried whispers. During the days, more would gather on the edge of the woods, or watch in groups high on the steep-sided valley, some daring to venture closer, but turning and running at the first sign of a drawn wand or witch's snarl.

It was Utharde's idea to one day leave a cauldron of steaming soup at the forest edge. She instructed a group of familiars to set it down by the nearest trees, before adding a ladle and large stack of wooden bowls. Nothing happened. At nightfall, she had the familiars light a fire under the cauldron to reheat the witchy broth, and gradually, under the cover of darkness, mysterious creatures finally appeared, cautiously ladling bowls of soup, tasting it, nodding, then encouraging others in the trees to join them and do the same.

Over the next month, the ritual was regularly repeated, both sides growing more confident in each other's company, until at last all could sit down together and try their best to communicate. Not a single wand was drawn that night, although many were turned in awed creatures' paws as they marvelled at the blue, glowing tips.

A creature with quite the longest nose Utharde had ever seen offered her a flagon of drink. She took a sip, grimaced and spat it out, coughing and wiping the back of her mouth.

"Guzzwort," he informed her.

Utharde, nodded, offering him a sip from her own flagon, watching as he squinted, choked and sucked in both cheeks. "Grimwagel wine. The witches' brew."

By the next morning, a large crowd of creatures had gathered to cautiously meet the witches and their familiars. The witches tried their best to be hospitable, but there seemed to be more arriving by the moment. Word had obviously spread, and although the creatures didn't appear in any way hostile, it was their sheer numbers that were threatening, some even beginning to arrive with large carts laden with tools and provisions. Utharde watched helplessly as they quickly began to organise themselves into groups, disappearing into the woods with axes to chop down trees and bring back as many building materials as possible. Small huts began springing up everywhere, the creatures happily singing as they went about their work, oblivious to the witches who lived there. By mid-afternoon, the meeting-house was surrounded in a dense ring of over fifty huts, creatures busily fetching food and firewood from the forest.

"This," Algorin quietly observed, "probably isn't quite what we had in mind."

Utharde nodded. "How can we stop it? We don't speak their language."

Algorin considered this. "Then we must learn," she said. "Either that, or we speak with our wands."

"You said they were never to be used in anger."

"Which is why we must learn." Algorin looked around the chaos of what had once been her home. "And not just their language. Look at their tools, Utharde, their methods. Creatures of all descriptions;

working together, helping one another. All without a single argument, curse or squabble." She took a breath. "These creatures are here to stay. We must accept that, or leave."

"And go where?" Utharde asked. "We have no idea what splurked dangers lie beyond these lands."

"Exactly," Algorin replied. "Our first journey was also our last. This is our home, Utharde – but now we must learn how to share it."

And learn they did. Slowly, at first, reluctantly, the lone survivors of The Great Crossing mostly trying their best to befriend the growing numbers of creatures who arrived to build their homes each and every day. Others resented any interaction at all, and would set off on their brooms at first light for the steep mountainsides, where they would spend the day suspiciously watching the activity below. Algorin wondered whether to try and coax them back down, but sensing their patience had been already tested by the journey, let them do as they pleased, simply glad her authority was still strong enough to keep the fragile peace.

It was like nothing the witches had ever seen before. All previous territorial disputes in The Howling Lands had started in daring raids and ended in terrible battles. This 'invasion' was something completely different. The sheer numbers and variety of creatures arriving each day made repelling it utterly futile. No amount of vrooshers would ever stop it, no matter how many of them tried.

And yet…it was all so peaceful. Not once had any of the creatures ever sought to harm the witches, merely showing a polite disinterest to the black-hatted sisters at most. And it was this that gave the strange creatures their strength, Algorin realised, their complete innocence of the witches' potentially violent ways. For even though some had witnessed the vrooshing power of a wand sail harmlessly above their heads, or thunder into the ground by their feet, none seemed to realise they'd cheated death by inches. It wasn't courage, stupidity or fearlessness. Neither was it any sort of cunning plan to frustrate the witches. It was simply the most blithe trust and wonderful innocence Algorin had ever seen.

Nor did the creatures seem impressed that witches could fly on brooms. At most, some might briefly look to the sky as a witch flew overhead, before getting back to building their homes.

"We must make them fear us," a frustrated witch announced in the meeting-house one night. "It is time to use our wands and show them the full majickal power they possess!"

The others all waited, turning to Algorin, some already gripping the wands around their waists.

She slowly pointed at the irate witch. "They do not fear what they cannot understand. Sister, when you can speak their language and tell them about vrooshers and our tzorkly-creed, you might discover you never have to show them the stroffing sting of your wand."

"Just one vroosher will tell them everything! They will leave in fear. We will have our lands back to ourselves."

"No," Algorin calmly replied. "You will have nothing but everything we all fought so hard to leave behind." She turned to the rest. "Those who wish to leave, take your brooms and do so now. But I warn you – fly far, far away. For if I see a single broom return, you will feel the sting of my wand!"

No one left, the outraged witch holding Algroin's eyeline for as long as she dared before slowly sitting back down.

"Good," Algorin smiled. "Then we learn, sisters. Each of us learns as much as we can about these creatures. I think they have far more to tell us than we could ever realise."

Algorin took the lead herself, encouraging groups of other witches to come with her as they went about the settlement, slowly getting to know certain of the creatures. Often they took small gifts they had foraged from the forest that the creatures would gladly accept before happily showing them their new homes and occasionally offering small trinkets in return.

After a long and largely happy summer, most of the witches had a working smattering of the creatures' language, surprised to find the ease at which they could speak it. Certain words and phrases were almost exactly alike. Certain meanings could be discerned from similar sounding words in their own tongue of Parlawitch. Other words (or 'griffles') had to be completely learnt from scratch. The language itself was called Dalespeak. Collectively, the creatures referred to themselves as 'Dales-Creatures' – although to have learned all their various species names would have taken more than a witch's lifetime in itself.

As autumn slowly turned to winter and the first snows fell, Algorin, the witches and the Dales-creatures were finally ready to feast together to celebrate a bountiful harvest. Initial communication was stilted, but as large barrels of guzzwort and Grimwagel wine were opened, slurred 'griff-versations' began flowing as readily as the drink itself. After, the witches shot their wands high into the night sky, letting off brooming vrooshers to massed cheers that echoed round the contented valley.

Less than ten years later, a community had peacefully grown by the river to become a teeming town of small streets and narrow alleys – all without a single argument or raised objection of any kind. It seemed the witches had finally found a peace they'd never reckoned on. However, history has never been one to seem satisfied by even the merest stilling of its progress, and as the governing engine of time played out through the mists of passing centuries and subsequent generations, the once peaceful town of Trasgar seemed to have another, quite different destiny planned for it…

VEYANOR

The Spuddle of Veyanor

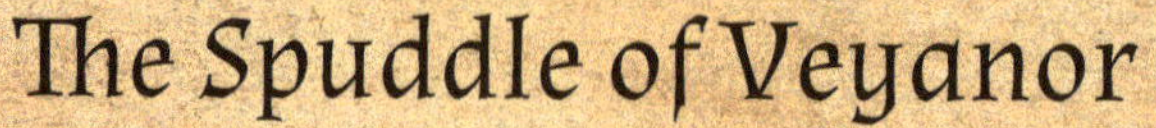

When we next arrive on the once hopeful riverbanks of Trasgar, much has changed. The town is almost unrecognisable in the four centuries since we last left it. New generations have replaced the original settlers, buildings torn down and replaced. Taller, stronger medieval townhouses now line the crowded streets, shuts and alleyways. There are markets, inns, taverns, blacksmiths, carpenters and a busy port with long wooden jetties pointing out into the river. Merchant barges continually arrive laden with goods, their sharp-eyed owners closely gripping valuable bags of trading drutts around their bloated waists.

Drutts – small pebbles of no real or actual worth that served as currency – changed the entire fabric of Trasgar. Some creatures grew rich from them, buying new boats and building large houses, whilst others with were left to beg without a single drutt to their name. In one of the greatest ironies of the Majickal Dales, not a single creature or witch ever thought to simply go to the riverbank and help themselves to the pebbles for free. All merely accepted that there were some who would always have them, some who would work for them, and others who would never feel the weight of even the tiniest drutt in their paw.

The merchants hadn't simply bought trade and drutts, though. Fearful of the vulnerability of their large and splendid homes, the rich traders quickly set about to create a system of law and order in which in all creatures and witches knew their place - namely in their own 'quarters' of the town patrolled by a garrison of Officious Krates, under the leadership of Thunke, Tresgar's very own Beadle.

Notorious short in both stature and temper, Thunke overrode his obvious physical deficiencies with the aid of a long conical hat and ever-expanding book of laws and regulations for his uniformed Officious Krates to enforce as he twirled his thick moustache. And whilst it would be fair to say that most of Thunke's rules were largely ignored by both creatures and witches, the one thing that was rigorously enforced were the towns' 'quarters' – the witches' being deemed the most important to keep contained.

Occupying a small maze of narrow, twisting streets, the witches' quarter was permanent home to the last surviving group of creature-witches. Numbering less than a hundred, these original descendants from The Great Crossing now lived a very different life from their 'tzorkly' ancestors. Banned from flying except within their own quarter, similar restrictions were also placed on wand vrooshing and spells of any kind. Penalties for infringements were as severe as Thunke and his Officious Krates could think of, which, fortunately for the witches mostly involved mild cases of public humiliation rather than anything more serious. Some historians suggest this showed a gentler, more moderate and forgiving side to the stout Beadle, whilst others say it merely demonstrated an immense lack of both leadership and imagination. For example, one 'punishment' meted out was to have your face dipped in a warm pie. Clearly, the assembled crowd enjoyed it, and on many occasions the prisoner was seen to do the very same, sometimes even licking her lips in anticipation of the imminent free meal.

For the witches and their familiars, life in the quarter was anything but 'tzorkly' or majickal. Made powerless, most days were spent simply making souvenirs and trinkets for the merchant families and their rich friends when they came visiting. Occasionally a merchant's wife might buy a hat or piece of hazel carved to look like a wand, the precious drutts quickly being traded for food. Small tours were conducted around the narrow streets, the witches expected to welcome visitors into their homes and recite an old spell around a bubbling cauldron and offer the chance to stir it with their long ladles. Or better still for younger, wide-eyed visitors, the chance to hit one of the suspended 'calling cauldrons' that now acted as bells high above the narrow streets.

Inevitably, as the years passed, the witches soon forgot about their own precious roots: Algorin, The Howling Lands and The Great Crossing fading with each generation. All except one witch – Veyanor, the quarter's broom-maker, and chief 'spuddle-teller' – destined by fate to become a legendary spuddle in her own right when the time came.

Which curiously, is precisely the very same time we first meet her...

The Visitor

Veyanor's day had been much like any other. Before dawn, she'd left the quarter, sneaking past sleeping Officious Krates and out into the woodland beyond the town to gather branches for her brooms. As ever, Herik, her crow familiar, perched on her shoulder looking for danger, his black eyes alert as she gathered sticks deep in the forest.

When she was done, she bundled them up and returned via her familiar route, carefully avoiding patrolling krates and slowly working her way back into the very centre of Trasgar, ducking down alleyways and slipping into the shadows for fear of being discovered. The ritual had become a daily quest – a journey to the one building she considered to be most sacred above all others. Most in the town would barely have noticed it, sandwiched in an ordinary row of unruly timber framed houses. Some nearby residents had complained it was too ugly, others that it was clearly falling down and the krates should finish the job and build something more fitting in its place. No one lived there. And apart from Veyanor, no one had ventured inside for many, many years. Because to do that, you had to know the secret. The door was hidden away slightly to the side of the rotting figurehead that hung down so awkwardly from the curved wooden roof. Some dales-creatures said the building had once been a boat used by witches to get to the Majickal Dales many centuries before. Most dismissed such nonsense with the contempt it deserved. The 'building' was simply a dangerous eyesore, and should be pulled down immediately.

But for Veyanor, the old Meeting House, once the proud tzorkly heart of Trasgar, was her true 'home'. Lured by tales she had heard whispered to her as a child of the brave group of witches who once sailed inside in the very same hull now rotting above her head, battling storms, dragons and sea-spiders, Veyanor's imagination took her travelling alongside them as she sat quietly in the gloom. Indeed, if she shut her eyes, she could almost hear the swell of the sea and the cries of her ancestors as they rode the waves. Oh, to have been there!

And whilst Veyanor sat, Herik would find his favourite perch inside the rotting hull, peering down at the door, keeping guard lest they be discovered. But on this day, something else caught his glinting black eye, wedged between one of the surviving cross beams. A small stone, perhaps no bigger than a drutt, but on its surface the cut symbol of a star. Carefully, he levered it out with his beak, then flapped to the floor, depositing it in Veyanor's lap. Frowning, she opened one eye and examined it in her paw, feeling its majick almost immediately and breaking into quite the largest smile Herik had ever seen. Silently ordering him up onto her shoulder, she quickly put the precious stone into her leather waist bag, gathered up her branches and made her way carefully back to the witches' quarter. Once there, she showed no one what she'd found, knowing that somehow it was a precious gift from the Ancestors themselves.

She spent the rest of the day making brooms and telling spuddles for visitors, anxious to once more be alone with her stone and hold its power. One or two other creature-witches noticed she appeared to be distant and distracted, but as they considered Veyanor to always have a 'head full of splurked spluddles', few paid her anymore attention than normal.

Come the evening, as other witches headed to the tavern to drink Grimwagel wine, Veyanor stayed in her own room, setting the stone on her windowsill in the light of the full moon, unable to stop looking at it, wondering at its history and majickal possibilities. She'd never seen anything like it, yet the markings surely meant it must have some sort of purpose. All of which thrilled her.

"It's a raven stone," came a sudden voice from behind.

Veyanor jumped, turning to be confronted by the oldest witch she'd ever seen.

"Don't be twizzled," the stranger said, holding out an arm that Herik gratefully settled on. "You've been chosen. You didn't find the stone – it found you."

"Who are you?" Veyanor managed to ask, mind racing. The old face

was truly twizzlyfying and looked like it had seen a hundred lifetimes. "Have you come to stroff me?"

The witch quietly chuckled. "I am an old friend you've never met. I've walked in the shadows for far too long, just like you have, waiting to meet you. I've seen you out in the woods, watched many times as made your way to the longboat, knowing all along that somehow you must be the *one* – the witch to follow in Algorin's sacred footsteps and resurrect the one thing we have all have lost over the ages – *The League of Lid-Curving Witchery.*"

Veyanor was speechless. Part of her wanted to run from the frightening creature, yet there was something kindly in her eyes that even Herik seemed completely comfortable with.

"My name," the old witch said, "is Utharde. I crossed The Icy Seas with Algorin. The raven stone once belonged to Ragnhilda, her mother. Its majick is all-powerful, and now it is yours." She held out hand for the stone. "Watch."

Veyanor watched Utharde take a small bag from her waist, spilling another twelve stones onto a small table.

"There are thirteen in all," Utharde explained, her elderly claws pointing to the symbols on each. "Together they can foretell destinies, and come together when they are needed the most. Twelve were lost at sea on our voyage. I've waited for many years, traveling far and wide to find each one as The Icy Seas slowly gave each one back up to me."

Veyanor finally found her voice. "So it's all true, the spuddle of Algorin and The Great Crossing?"

Utharde nodded, and for the next few hours the two of them talked, Veyanor listening in rapt attention as Utharde recalled the journey, life in The Howling Lands and the formation of the league.

"All that has been lost now," she eventually said. "But the great tzorkly spirit in which we undertook our journey has awoken, Veyanor, and my job here is done. I am an elderly witch, glad to finally hand these stones to their rightful owner." She took Veyanor's paw and squeezed it tightly. "When the time comes, you'll know what to do. Listen with your heart."

Veyanor looked down at the stones. "But how? How will I know?"

But when she looked up, the elderly witch was quite gone. Herik flapped onto the table, expectantly looking up at her.

"Well," she said, lightly stroking his feathered back. "We've had some pretty strange even'ups, you and I, but this has to be quite the oddest. Or should I say, most tzorkly?"

Later that night, as the witches' quarter slept, Veyanor's dreams were full of dragons, high seas and spectacular vrooshers streaking across heavy skies. She slept as the others in Trasgar slept that night – so deeply that nothing would wake them. Some hadn't slept as soundly in years. For others, it was the first time they'd ever dropped off so suddenly. Even those who loved the lure of the night's dark mysteries found themselves wrapped in deepest sleep. It was as if the whole of Trasgar had been majicked by something that had been waiting many years for the right opportunity to show itself.

Yet if any creature or witch had stirred, made their way blearily to the window and looked up into the clear night sky, they would have seen the most majestic of birds, gracefully emerging from behind a bright full moon, gliding and circling high over the town, its gleaming black eyes searching for one house above all others, the one individual who had been chosen to hear its wisdom…

Veyanor woke with a start, senses fully alert, drawn by insistent tapping at her window. Cautiously, she lit a candle and she made her way over, Herik already on the sill, his black beak trying to lift the catch.

"Who's there?" she asked, opening it. "Who calls me at this hour?"

She gasped as the magnificent raven in the small witches' hat showed itself.

"Idla?"

The bird elegantly flew onto a small table on the far side of the sparse room, its head nodding towards the hidden raven stones.

"You want me to cast them?" Veyanor asked, opening the bag. "Now?"

The bird nodded again.

"Utharde was here. She told me about you, the journey, Algorin and these stones."

The bird simply looked at the tabletop.

Swallowing, Veyanor cast the stones around Idla's feet, watching in silent fascination as the bird carefully scrutinised the patterns, its head turning from side to side, softly clicking and cawing. She cleared her throat. "What...do they say?"

Idla looked at her for a long time, examining her as carefully as the stones themselves, reading Veyanor's every thought, assessing the importance of the moment, determining if this quiet spuddle-telling witch could ever be up to the task before her. Seemingly content, she slowly opened her wings, flapped them vigorously, then flew from the room straight back out into the silent night.

"Well," Veyanor slowly said as Herik settled on her shoulder. "What have we here?"

It was a small, useless twig, left scattered in the middle of the stones, the kind she would so often discard when making her brooms. "I think perhaps Idla was having a most splurked joke with us, Herik."

She went to the window, closing it against the cold, and letting out a long breath.

Herik suddenly began to caw.

Lying on the table, the twig had begun to glow. Slowly at first, barely discernible, but the longer Veyanor looked, the brighter the ends became; first pink, then orange, to a final fiery red, shaking on the table until it finally jumped into the air and suddenly hurled itself against the window.

Veyanor instinctively knew what to do, grabbing the hot twig, ignoring the pain and racing outside to her broom maker's yard and quickly lashing it into the ends of her favourite flying broom. "Stay here," she commanded Herik. "Guard the stones. Let no one know of them."

He blinked, annoyed to be left out of what he clearly thought was the beginning of a most majickal adventure.

She sighed, mounting the broom, feeling its sudden, roaring power beneath her. "All right. You can come. But hold on, Herik. I've no idea where this is taking me!"

Gripping the broom, they took off into the night sky, Veyanor sucking her breath at the sheer speed. She'd never flown so fast. She whooped with the sheer exhilarating thrill of it, the broom flying far out from the town over steep-sided mountains, climbing ever-higher under a night sky alive with thousands of shimmering stars.

"There!" she suddenly shouted, pointing to a small black shape up ahead. "It's Idla! She's waiting for us."

Moments later the broom slowed almost to a stop, before suddenly swooping, diving and following Idla's every move as she gracefully soared through the night. Relaxing her grip slightly, Veyanor looked down, making out mountains, lakes, rivers and occasional lights and fires from settlements far, far below. "There are others here, Herik! Look. Not just Trasgar. Other towns, villages and creatures!"

The revelation stunned her. She'd never for a single moment thought her homelands to be so vast, stretching to and beyond every horizon. All she'd ever known was her hometown, its valley, woodlands and river. All that now paled into nothing. There were great mountain ranges, boundless forests, plateaus and soaring cliffs. It looked endless, almost impossible to take in. Whatever Veyanor may have thought she knew about her homelands she now knew to be completely insignificant.

Beyond the revelation was a growing excitement. Where was she going? Why had she been chosen? What was her purpose? Granted, it was her choice to bind the burning twig to her broom – but really, had it ever really been a 'choice' at all? Had Idla known all along that she'd follow? Had Utharde known the very same, and that by throwing the stones the great Soothwing would lead her on a new and tzorkly adventure? Too many questions. Yet Veyanor knew with every moment that somehow – inevitably – the answers were getting closer and closer…

The Vroffa-Tree Inn

Suddenly, Idla veered sharply to the left, the broom veering right and once again picking up colossal speed as it sped towards what looked like a solid mountainside and certain death. Veyanor instinctively tried all she could to slow it, her efforts quite futile. The broom knew exactly where it was going, its journey with the Idla over, the great bird never looking back as it elegantly flew away into the night.

"Hold on tight, Herik!" Veyanor shouted, feeling completely twizzled as the rocky mountainside reared up out of the darkness. "This is going to get splurked!"

She closed her eyes, bracing for the terrible impact, not knowing what or who to pray for, or even the words. Moments later everything turned inky-black, the roaring broom suddenly louder than ever before. She opened her eyes, took a huge breath and glanced back over her shoulder to see a tunnel entrance quickly disappear into the distance. They were inside the mountain! She cried out in relief, her voice barely heard above the twisting, turning broom. Occasionally, she'd catch a glimpse of a flaming torch flash by where differing tunnels intersected as the broom flew on, clearly knowing exactly where it was going. And what tunnels they were! Some tight as a coil and dizzyingly endless, some completely straight, plunging deeper and deeper into the heart of the mountain, before suddenly twisting, Veyanor clinging to the broom for all she worth, chin to the handle to avoid the low roof.

At last, they began to slow, the tunnels gradually becoming lighter. She took a deep breath, looking up ahead at a welcoming orange glow. A series of flaming torches lined the tunnel wall on each side before it suddenly opened out into quite the most enormous cavern she'd ever seen.

"Grodelshammen!" she gasped. "You could fit the whole of Trasgar in here!"

The broom carried them over a vast lake that filled the cave towards a small island in the very middle. A ring of trees circled a single building, smoke pouring from the chimney and laughter ringing out from inside.

Herik climbed onto Veyanor's shoulder as they slowly approached. High above, other witches whooped and cackled as they circled the cavern roof, letting fly with vrooshers from their wands as they dodged and chased each other around vast hanging stalactites. Veyanor's eyes widened. Other witches? She'd never even thought of such a thing, but now as the broom gently descended onto the island and landed on the well-kept lawn between the trees and the building, she saw more witches sitting on benches, talking and laughing, jugs of Grimwagel wine in their hands, and a large stack of brooms propped against the wall by a heavy wooden front door.

"Welcome," a friendly voice said. "Welcome to The Vroffa Tree Inn."

Veyanor turned to be greeted by a smiling creature with large paws holding a clutch of empty wooden wine jugs. She wore an apron, headscarf, had a long nose and quite the most piercing eyes Veyanor had seen. Whoever this curious creature was, she seemed to know all about Veyanor. "Who are you?"

"I am Laffrohn," the smiling creature answered. "Landlady and keeper of the most majickal inn in all the Majickal Dales; The Vroffa Tree Inn."

Nearby, a group of witches were beginning to take an unhealthy interest in the visitor, talking amongst themselves, nodding, hissing and pointing. However welcoming the landlady appeared, all Veyanor's instincts told her to leave and try and find her way back.

"You wouldn't last but a few blinksnaps if you tried," Laffrohn gently chuckled. "The broom would bring you right back here."

"Blinksnaps?"

"The time it takes to blink an eye. The smallest moment – or as we would say the 'oidiest' moment."

"I'm not sure what you mean, or what I'm doing here," Veyanor replied, aware the group of witches were now gradually encircling them.

Laffrohn smiled. "Oh, I think you know *exactly* why you be here, Veyanor. And truth is, I've been waiting for some time, too." She turned to the witches, raising a small, frizzing wand. "Any of you that wants to feel the sting of this, just try taking one step closer."

The witches growled, slowly backing away.

"Sisters of The Crooked Hats coven," Laffrohn explained, chuckling. "All talk and no vrooshing. Always been the way with them. Now, shall we step inside somewhere a little more hospitable? You must be thirsty after your journey. How about a nice mug of the old Grimwagel, eh?"

Veyanor nodded, unsure, but somehow trusting the strange creature who could so easily twizzle such a fearsome bunch of witches. She looked at their hats, noticing that indeed each was crooked or twisted in some way. But a whole coven of them? Merely because they all wore splurked hats? It just seemed so ridiculous. Not that she'd ever dare tell them, for regardless of Laffrohn's confidence that they'd never draw a wand they looked like the very last witches she'd ever want to tangle with. Steeling herself, she followed the landlady, still clutching her broom, Herik's talons tightly gripping onto her shoulder.

At the door Laffrohn pointed to the large stack of broomsticks. "Leave yours here. You'll need it later. Don't worry, it will find you."

"Can I ask...?"

"How I know your name?"

Veyanor nodded.

"And also how I knew you were going to ask that very same question?"

Veyanor nodded again.

Laffrohn thought about it. "No," she simply said, opening the heavy wooden door. "You may not."

And with that, she disappeared inside, Veyanor leaving the broom and quickly following into a riot of noise. She'd never seen so many rowdy creature-witches in one place at a time. The whole inn was packed. Some sung, some danced on the tables, others vrooshed hats off with their wands, streaking blue bouncing off wooden roof beams to sting others with a loud pop. At the centre was a large bar where more witches clamoured for Grimwagel wine, crying out to be served, empty wooden jugs held high in the air. To the side, a large cauldron boiled over what was the largest blazing hearth Veyanor had ever seen, its flickering light shimmering across the entire inn. Dozens of thick heavy candles burnt on tables, wall fixings and ceiling chandeliers, the hot wax freely dripping on those below. It really was unlike any tavern Veyanor had visited in the witches' quarter in Trasgar.

She followed Laffrohn closely, marvelling at how easily the landlady parted the seething scrum. Just who was this creature? Who were all these other witches? Why on earth had Idla seen fit to bring her to such a twizzly place? Nothing made any sense – yet for once, far away from Trasgar, everything was simply *exciting* and that, for Veyanor, was the quite best and most unexpected of all feelings. Grinning, she pinched herself as she made her way through the crowd. No, she wasn't dreaming. It was all wonderfully, chaotically real.

At the bar, she was amazed to see just one small witch flying on a broom serving the boisterous crowd. The tiny witch confidently took each jug, flew to the large Grimwagel barrels, filled them from a small wooden tap, before returning them to its gleeful owners. She must have been no bigger than Veyanor's hand, yet managed with a ferocious efficiency that told of many such years in the job.

"You're surprised?" Laffrohn asked as she lead Veyanor behind the bar. "Just because Brutel's an oidy-witch, doesn't mean she's not the best witch to run this bar."

"Peffa-oidy witch, actually," the tiny witch retorted as she flew past with another jug. "It means 'very small'."

"I'll try and remember that," Yeyanor said above the throng.

"Please do," Brutel replied, filling another jug. "Or I'll have to vroosh you. I may have a peffa-oidy wand – but it's got the most twizzly sting."

"I don't doubt it for a blinksnap," Veyanor muttered, trying to avoid catching anyone's eye. There were so many witches pressing at the bar, yet the longer she looked, the more she began to notice similarities between them. Some wore crooked hats, others dressed quite smartly, their robes elaborately embroidered. One group had dark green robes, hats and elaborately painted faces with leaves, trees and plants weaving right across in intricate patterns. Whist another groups robes looked to be made from course brown sacking, their waists hung with thick leather belts heavy with strange tools and wands.

"The four covens of the Majickal Dales," Laffrohn explained, pointing at each in turn. "The Crooked Hats, you already know."

"All wands and no vrooshers," Veyanor confirmed.

"Exactly," Laffrohn nodded. Next, she pointed to the smartly embroidered witches. "Those be the Lid Sisters. The best flyers, who think just because they're smart on a broom, it be giving them the right to look down on the rest of us, too." She playfully nudged Veyanor in the ribs. "Get far too big for their fancy hats, they do."

"And those?" Veyanor asked, pointing to the green robed witches.

"The Earth Weavers; sisters of plants, herbs and potions. They look quite mild, but some of their practices can be most twizzly indeed." Lastly, Laffrohn pointed to the final group. "See those with all the wands and belts? They're the Bindnapps, makers of things. If you want a new cauldron, wand or almost anything else, visit a Bindnapp and she'll make you one. But be careful of the price, mind, as chances are it'll most likely cost you more than you could ever imagine."

"I don't doubt it," Veyanor replied. "I just never for a blinksnap imagined there's be so many other witches, other covens. It never even occurred to me."

Laffrohn chuckled. "Stuck away in Trasgar? That's no surprise. See, the thing that's always all too easy to forget – wherever you may be, whatever you are, whatever you be doing – is that you're the only one. 'Tis the folly of so much of all of it. And 'tis also why travel be the best thing for the broadening of the mind. Too many folks simply get stuck simply believing their lives are all there is, and that nothing majickal lies beyond. When really, so much more awaits those who choose to venture forth with an open heart." She looked at Veyanor. "But a part of you already knew this long ago, didn't it? 'Tis simply that finally you chose to listen. And now that you have, now that you're here, you'll soon discover many more things about the Majickal Dales that you never knew existed besides just these four covens."

CROOKED HATS
Grimwagel horn
Trickster's Smile
Splurked Wand
Sturdy boots for crash landings

The Crooked Hats

The largest of the four covens, Crooked Hats are found in unhealthy numbers in all the Majickal Dales. The members themselves will tell you they're also the oldest of all four covens – but then again, Crooked Hats like nothing more than to exaggerate about almost anything to start pointless arguments they will also always claim to 'win', thanks to having no ear-holes in their hats to listen to your side of things.

Perhaps the most obvious question to ask is 'Why the crooked-hats?' Again, don't rely on coven members to give you anything other than a splurked explanation, especially if they've had more than two horns of Grimagel wine. The *actual* reason is lost in the tzorkly mists of time, but the popular reason derives from when these witchy-tricksters caused so much general annoyance it would frequently end in their hats being violently twisted by other fuming witches. Over time, they grew to accept their ruined hats as a badge of cunning and guile, and subsequently even began splurking their *own hats* to let other covens know just whom they were dealing with.

Perhaps the worst of all flyers, Crooked Hats are prone to frequent splurked landings and in-flight catastrophes (especially after too much Grimwagel) and often wear reinforced toecaps on their boots to minimise their many scrapes and accidents.

You may well wonder just what (if any) redeeming factors these rather obstreperous witches have. Few have ever really bothered to find out – but if you did manage to tolerate their boisterous, sometimes infantile behaviour, you'd find that like most of us, all they really want is to be accepted and liked for what they are; great company for an unforgettable night out, loyal friends never short of a prank, and – if you can tolerate their untidiness and complete lack of practical skills – witches that can sometimes bring the most precious of all things, a smile to your face as you rediscover your own lost playful-youth that may well have been long-forgotten.

The Earth Weavers

The most secretive of all four covens, Earth Weavers are also the smallest, both in stature and numbers. But here, it would be folly to underestimate their true importance, prowess or majickal powers. Distinct with their long hair, antlers and deep robe pockets full of herbs, roots, plants and flowers for tincture making, Earth Weavers are notoriously difficult to find, mostly only emerging from their burrows in the moonlight to forage for the precious assets that they'll take back and mix in their cauldrons in timeless recipes and potions.

Inevitably, Earth Weavers are often sought by other creature-witches when they need herbal treatments for various ailments. Often, the sheer numbers of witches seeking treatment can be overwhelming for the smaller Earth Weaver, hence some will employ the services of several willing Crooked Hats to guard their burrow entrances in exchange for a horn or two of Grimwagel wine. Further, it's been noted that these particular Crooked Hats are nearly always ailment-free, as if by merely standing by the entrance, they immediately benefit from the amount of healing majick inside.

Payment for Earth Weavers is by way of charms in return for potions or rune-stone readings, and here it's wise to ensure the charm is something she'll appreciate, lest you want to feel the very painful sting of her small, but powerful wand! However, most Earth Weaver's temperaments are quite calm, mirroring the changes of the four seasons that see the earth replenished to give again the following year. Of all the four covens, Earth Weavers are also considered the most creative and artistic, frequently fashioning beautiful art-works from nature's own raw materials: snow, leaves, bark, flowers, shrooms, rocks and stones. Some say they do this purely for the joy of the moment, others that the works have special, majickal significances – but either way, the Earth Weavers, who rarely fly and keep their bare feet very much on the ground, also keep the true purpose of such works very much to themselves. Which, if you ever got to know one, would come as no real surprise…

EARTH WEAVERS
Hazel Wand
Majickal Antlers
Foraging Apron

LID SISTERS

Streamlined hat
Embroidered robes
Superior fingers
Racing boots

The Lid Sisters

Completely insistent they be recognised as the most important of all the four covens, Lid Sisters make no bones of constantly looking down on others, whether it be from far up on a broom, or with both expensively fashionable shoes on the ground. Indeed, with the Majickal Dales mostly trading in drutts, they're also no strangers to boasting about their wealth, or showing off their latest robes and wands at almost every social event they can.

Such a lifestyle, however, can have tragic and fatal consequences, as jealousies between who is the richest or most lavishly attired frequently spill over into fantastic aeronautical duals as differences are settled high in the clouds, the winner entitled to all the deceased's drutts and belongings.

Yet for all their conceited and often dangerous snobbery, no witch can deny the aerial superiority of The Lid Sisters, and it would be a fool who would try to better one on her broom. Taller and thinner than other witches, their hats bent back for streamlining, Lid Sisters begin flying before they can even walk. The Twinkling Lid is their 'real' home, and whilst their houses are just as ostentatious as you'd expect, this is simply to impress their peers, as they much prefer to spend their time learning new tricks and exploring the Majickal Dales high up on their brooms. Also, with their uniquely cultured voices, they make for the best arbiters in inter-coven disputes, most witches deferring to a Lid Sister's verdict simply because it *sounds* right, and they don't have to be bothered to make the decision themselves.

The average Lid Sister will have a collection of well over a hundred separate brooms for different occasions, but woe betide anyone foolish enough to dare to ask to ride one – a splurked strategy that will result in instant stroffing!

Bindnapps

Motto: *It's the makers that truly shape the future.*

Bindnapps are makers of things. Whatever you require, there'll be a Bindnapp who'll fashion it for you. Living in small cottages surrounded by mountains of old scrap and useless junk; Bindnapps are highly skilled in not only using, but also making tools of all descriptions. They can just as easily carve you a new wand as forge a cauldron set complete with cast-iron tripod stand and fire-grid. But – here's the important point to remember – at a price.

Bindnapps, by their very practical nature, have neither a belief or need for drutts. No amount of the worthless pebbles could buy you even the smallest potion-rack. Instead, the Bindnapp will ask you for a threefold return on what she perceives to be the value of the item in your life. And you'll have three moon-turns (or months) to repay her. If your new wand makes you able to vroosh more accurately, the Bindnapp will demand something that also makes her life three times easier, also. Most witches get around this thorny problem by visiting a second Bindnapp to fashion such a device to repay their original debt. However, then they will have to visit a third Bindnapp for the very same reason, then a fourth, and so on – until they are caught in a most splurked 'bind' – hence the entirely appropriate name.

However, all is not lost. The other way to potentially repay a Bindnapp is via Grimwagel wine in the local tavern. After a few tankards, most will agree to more reasonable terms, providing you're willing to spend the evening listening to their many tales, spuddles and tall-stories. However, this strategy isn't without danger. Never ask a Bindnapp where they acquired their many unusual tools, and under no circumstances make any reference to another Bindnapp's work being superior to theirs. However much wine they've had, no Bindnapp will ever admit anyone is anywhere near as good as them, and such clumsy conversations frequently end very badly for everyone in the tavern at the time!

BINDNAPPS

Pincushion hat
Canny eyes
Zorkly tool belt
Tough Leather Jurkin

Before Veyanor could ask any more, Laffrohn clapped her large paws and ordered everyone to quieten down. Impressively, they all did, some scowling and grumpily shoving each other, but fairly shortly, the entire inn had settled into a more or less respectful silence.

"Sisters," she announced. "We have ourselves a visitor tonight. She's come from far away, and we need to be extending to her our every courtesy."

No one seemed particularly keen on the idea.

"What coven's she from?" one witch suspiciously asked.

"How she get here?" another hissed.

A tall, elegantly dressed Lid Sister pointed at Veyanor with a long, bony finger. Her voice was calm, measured, and yet full of cold hostility. "The peace amongst our four covens is extremely fragile. I strongly suggest you fly back to whatever squalid cave you came from and never venture back. That is, if you value your wretched little life."

Laffrohn simply smiled at Veyanor, nodding at her to speak.

She cleared her throat in the heavy silence. "Believe me, I had no urge to come here. I was given a majickal branch by Idla. Then my broom flew me from Trasgar, and..."

She got no further, the inn erupting into a chorus of mocking jeers.

"Trasgar?" a grinning Bindnapp shouted out. "Never heard of no place like it. You be making it up! I say we stroff her!"

"Idla?" an Earth Weaver cried. "That glopped, splurked bird is just an old spuddle! There be no such thing! You'll be telling us that all the foolish talk about Algorin and The Great Crossing be true, next!"

"But it is," Veyanor tried over the rising laughter. "All of it. The boat is still there, in Trasgar. I visit it every day. Utharde came to me, Idla bought me here."

The Lid Sister swiftly held up a hand, silencing the inn. Clearly, she also commanded as much respect as Laffrohn. "Why?"

"Sorry?" Veyanor gulped.

"Why, if what you say is true, would Idla ever visit *you*?" She looked Veyanor up and down. "A frankly rather vulgar splurk who seems to think that simply having a scruffy crow on her shoulder somehow makes her credible."

Herik cawed at her, narrowing his black eyes. Veyanor calmed him. "I have no idea why she chose me. I am just a spuddle-teller and broom maker. My life is probably nowhere as near majickal or exciting as yours – but perhaps the simple fact is that I *believed*."

The witch shook her head, tutting. "All you believed, sister, was one of your own splurked spuddles. I am Bethgella, the finest flier here. Several times I have ventured far out to Trasgar. I've looked down and seen your witches' quarter where you live like specimens to amuse the other creatures. You – and the others like you – are nothing more than an entertainment." She stopped, silently thinking, sliding her tongue over her large teeth. "And yet, if you are what you say you are, and have some sort of majickal broom, surely you'd also be able to beat me in a flying contest, wouldn't you?"

Laffrohn broke the silence. "Bethgella, if our visitor wins, then you'll give her respect and listen to what she has to say?"

The witch laughed. "Wins?"

Laffrohn whispered into Veyanor's ear. "Clap your paws three times."

"Why?"

"Just do it."

Veyanor did, amazed when the heavy wooden door swung open and her broom sailed over everyone's heads at the bar and straight into her open paw.

Even Brutel nodded, appreciatively. "Not bad. For a beginner."

"Now then, Bethgella," Laffrohn teased, "just what kind of a contest would be talking about? Seems like the stranger here is more than ready to take to the lid."

Bethgella frowned. "Cheap tricks, Laffrohn."

The other witches mumbled amongst themselves. "What's it to be then, Bethgella?"

"A race," she announced. "To the Raising Stone and back!"

The inn erupted in cheers, Veyanor anxiously looking at Laffrohn. "I've no idea where that is."

"Doesn't matter," Laffrohn smiled, pointing at the broom, the majick twig already glowing bright red. "The broom knows. Now get outside, climb on, hold on tight – and win!"

Moments later, Veyanor was swept outside with the eager crowd. Laffrohn took Herik from her shoulder. "I've been waiting a long time for this," the landlady told her. "Win, and you revive *The League of Lid-Curving Witchery* and all it once stood for."

"And if I lose?"

Laffrohn chuckled. "How can you? You believe, you're tzorkly – it's why Idla and the Ancients chose you."

"Who are you?" Veyanor asked as the broom began to roar. "Really?"

But before Laffrohn could answer Bethgella had set off up into the vast cavern roof, Veyanor's broom instantly following as the whole cavern filled with wild cheers, vrooshers streaking out into the echoing darkness.

On her broom, Veyanor clung on harder than ever before, racing for the roof, eyes shut as it spun, rocked and twisted through the dangling forest of dripping stalactites, before suddenly veering left into a tunnel entrance flagged by two burning torches. Bethgella was nowhere to be seen, either already far ahead, or having taken another tunnel. Veyanor simply trusting to the broom as it tore through the matrix of tight turns, wincing as she felt the ends of her shoes perilously scrape against cold rock.

Now, more than ever, she had to believe in all the spuddles, legends and stories so often mocked and laughed at by others. Flying at reckless speed on a broom with its own majickal will, Veyanor desperately hoped that for whatever reason she'd been chosen for such a splurked adventure, she'd be able to please the Ancients. Eyes tightly shut, she saw many things: Algorin standing by her mother's figurehead, the sea-spiders, the storm and the dragon – all as she heard a strange new voice...

> *As above, so below – to the Raising Stone you'll go,*
> *Fly like the wind and your name they'll know,*
> *Veyanor, spuddle-teller, tzorkly sister of the lid,*
> *For saving the sacred league is what she did.*

She opened her eyes as suddenly the wind burst all round, violently rocking the broom. She was out in the open! In front, she make out a large mountain in the darkness, and from it another small figure emerging and flying straight towards her, sending a streaking blue vroosher that just missed her hat. With no wand, Veyanor simply had to cling on as the broom suddenly dived, Bethgella cackling in the night as she roared overhead, turned and sent two more deadly vrooshers arrowing after Veyanor.

Ahead, the mountain plateaued to a level area, and in the exact centre stood quite the largest boulder Veyanor had ever seen – the Raising Stone. In moments, she was upon it, streaking around the back and setting back the way she'd come, Bethgella far too close behind.

"Think you can beat me, witch?" Bethgella screamed, blasting out another vroosher that tore a hole clean through Veyanor's hat. "You'll stroff, first!"

But the broom had other ideas, veering away and plunging down, before tearing through a thundering waterfall and up into a dripping tunnel. Behind, Bethgella cursed as she flew through the heavy wall of water, shocked by its power and tumbling from her broom to crash against the walls and drop onto the wet rock. Dazed, she stood, amazed to see Veyanor return, stop and offer a hand.

"Get on," Veyanor ordered, punctured hat still smoking from the vroosher. "Unless you really want to walk these tunnels by yourself."

Bethgella scowled. "In the first instance, no witch can ever walk the tunnels. They're mirrit-tunnels – to even set one foot on them would instantly stroff us."

"And the second instance?"

"I'm driving. Move over."

But Veyanor shook her head and prepared to roar off. Bethgella cursed and reluctantly climbed onto the back.

"These tunnels can stroff us?"

"You have much to learn about the Majickal Dales," Bethgella scowled.

"Indeed, I do," Veyanor smiled. "And I shall very much enjoy every oidy bit of it."

Before Bethgella could utter another word or curse, they both shot deep into the pitch-black tunnel.

At The Vroffa Tree Inn there was much revelry when the two witches returned. Bethgella was forced to reluctantly tell the others how she had been saved by the stranger, the inn swiftly applauding this and raising tankards of Grimwagel wine to Veyanor. Even those who'd first seemed hostile now appeared keen to celebrate the stranger's victory, as Laffrohn and Brutel expertly kept everyone's flagons filled.

After an hour Laffrohn reached up with her own wand from behind the bar and rang a large cauldron hanging over her head. "Sisters!" she announced as the room gradually quietened. "Truly, it has been a most memorable even'up. Our stranger is a stranger no more, and from this blinksnap will be known to us all as Veyanor."

Veyanor smiled as the room applauded, beginning to feel quite at home in this most curious of places.

"So which coven will you join?" a Bindnapp by her side asked her. "'Tis the question that vexes all of us. And just because you be most proficient on a broom, you don't have to be a Lid Sister. Remember, you're also a maker of things, too."

"And a spuddle teller," an Earth Weaver added, belching loudly after too much wine. "Our coven places much store in all the old spuddles. A good teller would be welcome amongst us. Why don't you join us?"

A Crooked Hat pushed her way forwards. "And if you like hats, especially splurked ones, we'd be happy to have you wearing one with us."

Veyanor laughed, thanking them all. "Such kind offers. And without wishing to offend I must confess that I already belong to a coven; perhaps one of the oldest and most forgotten. I think I'm probably its only surviving sister, too - The League of Lid-Curving Witchery."

"Never heard of it," a Bindnapp called out. "Sounds splurked, and the name be too much of a mouthful, for a start."

"Then perhaps," Laffrohn called out over the laughter, "you could all do with a little elucidation."

"Never heard of that, neither!" the Bindnapp replied. "Sounds like something right painful to me."

Laffrohn sighed, turning to Veyanor. "Forgive them," she said. "They don't get out too much. Perhaps you could educate them?"

So, for the next hour, Veyanor held the entire inn in rapt attention as she told them all she knew of the League: its origins in The Howling Lands, Algorin, Utharde, Idla and the perilous adventure across The Icy Seas. No one uttered a word during the telling, caught in all the spuddles, as Laffrohn and Brutel once again silently went from table to table, refilling tankards.

"So you see," Veyanor eventually said, "although I'd be more than humbled to join any one of your covens, I'd much prefer it if we all combined to make one League of Lid-Curving Witchery, as I'm now more certain than ever it's what the Ancients would really want."

"But how?" a Crooked Hat frowned. "I can't suddenly just give up a whole life of wearing splurked hats and being hostile for no reason. 'Tis in my very bones, passed to me by my equally hostile forebears. It would surely be a betrayal to be anything other than a Crooked Hat. Who amongst us here would give up the very essence of what we are to become part of something else?"

The others murmured and nodded in quiet agreement.

Laffrohn quietly surveyed the room. "Maybe," she suggested. "You could be both." She turned to them all. "Maybe you can all be both, still members of your own covens but also part of the one league. After all, 'tis surely the spirit of being tzorkly that binds all sisters together, no matter what coven they belong to?"

The witches silently considered this.

Pressing what she sensed might be an advantage in the lull, Laffrohn quickly ordered them all outside into the garden. There, she retrieved the majickal branch from Veyanor's broom and gently brushed it against the trunk of each tree that circled the inn as the others watched, confused.

"These be majickal vroffa-trees," she declared, her voice echoing in the huge cavern. "From now on, their branches will give you extra tzorkly majick for all of your brooms."

The witches watched as the ends of each branch of each tree gradually began to glow a fiery red.

"Every year, you can return here and take some new vroffa-branches for your brooms. They'll give you extra speed when you fly. But if any are used for splurked or hostile acts, they will fail you. They are a gift from the Ancients, and as such, you will honour it both as coven members and proud sisters of *The League of Lid Curving Witchery.* Now, take to your brooms, bind on some vroffa, fly out to your homelands and tell all other creature-witches what has happened here tonight – the night you all became part of The Spuddle of Veyanor."

The witches quickly set to, climbing the trees, breaking the glowing branches and binding them to their brooms. Soon the entire cavern was filled with ear-shattering roars as the witches flew up and away into the tunnels, yelping and whooping at new ferocious speeds.

After, Laffrohn showed Veyanor back inside the now empty inn. "I have something for you," she said, reaching behind Grimwagel barrels at the back of the bar. "It wasn't just the raven stones that were washed ashore. During the storm, Algorin's boat also lost an oar. A part of it has been here for many generations. Perhaps it was simply waiting for the right witch to own it." She pulled out a long shaft of wood. "Mind, I've made a few changes to it over the years. Just a hunch."

Veyanor gasped when she saw what was once the oar – now transformed into a witch's broom, complete with an elaborate dragon's head carved onto the front.

"I'm thinking you'll have many an adventure on this," Laffrohn smiled. "First it crossed The Icy Seas, now it'll be off on new travels in the twinkling-lid. As above, so below – a truly tzorkly broom."

Veyanor held it in her arms, scarcely able to believe it had once been used by Algorin and her courageous fellow travellers. "It's..."

"Saztaculous?" Laffron teased. "But more importantly, it be waiting for some vroffa for you to start its next tzorkly journey. You have much to do, Veyanor; four covens need governing and the witches need saving from the splurked quarter of yours in Trasgar. I don't think you've a blinksnap to lose."

They walked outside, Veyanor binding vroffa branches into her

broom and instantly feeling the roaring power in her hands.

"Don't fret," Laffrohn laughed. "It's perfectly safe, and will bring you back whenever you want."

Veyanor climbed on, the broom already desperate to leave. "There's so much I need to ask you."

"I know," Laffrohn replied. "But really, I think you know most of the answers already, don't you?"

And before she could say another word, the broom took off and sped away across the cavern into the dark tunnels and out into whatever lay beyond...

Throughout her long life, Veyanor went on to achieve many majickal and tzorkly things including liberating the witches of Trasgar, settling awkward disputes between the four covens, establishing *The League of Lid-Curving Witchery* rituals to mark important annual and seasonal celebrations, and perhaps most impressively, gaining acceptance and respect amongst dales-creatures of all descriptions. Witches were no longer thought of as simply raucous, wand-wielding, twizzly sisters – but as creatures in their own right, with their own majick, customs and culture.

By the time the Ancients called her, Veyanor was widely recognised as the first *Grand Tzorkly High Priestess of The League of Lid-Curving Witchery*, and whilst many others would follow, few would have the far-reaching impact she did.

However, for all her tzorkly achievements, the solution to one problem had always eluded her – solitary witches. Scattered throughout the Majickal Dales, these witches continued to keep themselves to themselves, intensely suspicious of the four covens, the League and all its activities. However much Veyanor was congratulated on her achievements, she also knew deep in her tzorkly heart that without the full participation of the solitary witches, *The League of Lid-Curving Witchery* would never achieve its true majickal potential.

It would take one very special witch before it was finally and spectacularly reached...

The League
Finally Becomes...
Solitaries, familiars
and the Spuddle of Sinchkin

History shows that the emergence of any new culture or civilisation is never without its splurked sticking points, and the same is true of *The League of Lid Curving Witchery* as with many such similar instances. Whilst some rush forward to greet the new dawn of change with open arms, others shy away into the shadows, fearful of its consequences, resentful of its presence.

Such was the case for the solitary witches of the Majickal Dales. Outsiders, shunned by each of the four covens, solitaries were treated with more or less the same hostility as Ragnhilda in The Howling Lands many centuries previously. Whilst they were unlikely to meet the same grisly fate in a boiling cauldron, nonetheless solitary witches knew full well that to be surrounded and captured by any of the four covens was to be avoided at all costs. Humiliating rituals, caging and burning down their small woodland hovels was commonplace, the solitary witch only finally released when the others had done with her, casting her out to try and resume whatever life she could far, far away.

It was a problem Veyanor had wrestled with for much of her time as *Grand Tzorkly High Priestess*. Her wish, to create a truly united league, was always frustrated by both the solitaries' natural reluctance to join, and the four covens' hostility towards them. The whole problem seemed quite intractable. Plus, being solitary, no one ever knew just how many there really were, or if they had any sort of leader. And with such dangerous levels of persecution, even finding the constantly moving witches was a huge task in itself, Veyanor knowing full well that if even one was tracked down, it was unlikely she would be bought before her, as there was too much splurked fun to be had with the unfortunate creatures instead.

In one final effort, Veyanor decreed that rewards would be offered for each solitary witch bought to her unharmed. Her intention was to be able to spend time explaining just what *The League of Lid-Curving Witchery* meant, and hopefully encourage other solitary witches to join. However, she also knew full well that the success of the scheme relied upon each of the four covens agreeing to the idea because they truly believed it to be *right* – rather than just an easy path to rewards. The first ten witches bought before her were quite obviously coven imposters badly disguised to look like solitaries.

Towards the end of her life, wearying of the problem, Veyanor had to accept that despite her best intentions, no single witch could be the one who changed everything. Gradually, she realised that like Algorin, she had merely been a stepping-stone. It would be up to another to finally combine all the witches of the Majickal Dales into one, all embracing league. Who that would be, when it would happen, how it would come about, she had no idea – yet somewhere within herself knew that it *would* happen, but not within her lifetime.

On the night she passed to the Ancients, Veyanor took to her bed in the large building that now stood as the league's central Meeting Hall. As a structure it was quite splendid, a testament to the combined skills of all four covens. The Bindnapps had built it, the Lid Sisters conceived the lavish design, the Crooked Hats worked as Bindnapp labourers, and the Earth Weavers had infused the building with special majick. When finished, it was considered so special, it attracted the attentions of many dales-creatures, who travelled long distances to bask in awe at its splendour. Together, they stood and marvelled at the witches' feat; amazed that such a building was even possible. Some even began cautiously employing the services of Bindnapps themselves, something the resourceful makers were only too glad to agree, as dales-creatures were frequently far more stupid than fellow witches, and hence easier to manipulate for the inevitable 'bind' they'd soon find themselves in.

Yet generally, the meeting hall served its purpose admirably, not only as a majickal place for tzorkly ritual and governance of all four covens, but also in forging links between witches and dales-creatures as a cautious trust between all parties slowly grew. Indeed, twice a year, on the summer and winter solstice, a great festival was held for both the dignitaries of each majickal dale and representatives of each coven. There, over two days of feasting, with Veyanor presiding, agendas were decided and disputes settled – mostly without too many splurked incidents.

But on Veyanor's final night in the hall, the mood was more sombre. Some amongst those gathered feared for the future. What would happen once she had passed to the Ancients? How long would the fragile truce between dales-creatures and witches last? Who would become next Grand Tzorkly High Priestess? Summoning the four coven leaders to her bedchamber, Veyanor painfully raised herself and spoke.

"It was always my intention," she told them, "to be nothing more than a spuddle-teller and broom maker. Those days are, of course, many moon-turns ago. Idla and the Ancients called me from Trasgar for a higher purpose, showing me lands I'd never imagined, friends I'd never met and opportunities I never could have believed existed. And now, as fate decrees, I too have been called, and will shortly leave on my final journey. My one regret is that our fellow solitary witches have declined to join our league, friendship and fellowship." She looked at the four hushed faces. "I have one more duty left to perform. The choosing of the next Grand Tzorkly High Priestess who will take my place."

They all bowed gracefully.

Veyanor first addressed the elegant Lid Sister. "Bethgella, whilst you are unbeatable on a broom, the next Grand Tzorkly High Priestess will also have to keep both feet very much on the ground. Step back, you have not been chosen."

Bethgella did so, trying not to scowl too obviously.

Veyanor turned to the Crooked Hat. "Pruttel, whilst you enjoy your fun and splurked jokes, the next Grand Tzorkly High Priestess will also have to know when to shed tears for her subjects, too. Step back."

Pruttel shrugged. "Rather glad, really," she admitted. "I'd have been a really splurked high priestess."

Next, Veyanor addressed the leader of the Earth Weavers. "Alfloria, the next Grand Tzorkly High Priestess will not only need a heart for nature's majick, but also a head to make the practical decisions and ears to listen to the wisdom of the Ancients. Unfortunately, you have neither."

Alfloria reluctantly stepped back, shooting a look at the last witch, the leader of the Bindnapps, who was already beaming expectantly.

"Before you get too excited, Teghart," Veyanor warned her, "it's not you either. Saztaculous maker of things you may be, but the next Grand Tzorkly High Priestess will also have to make plans, alliances, peace and decisions – and none of your tools will help you with those."

It was Bethgella who broke the awkward silence. "So, may I ask just who *will* be our next Grand Tzorkly High Priestess? If not one of us, then who?"

Veyanor nodded, her elderly eyes slowly closing as somewhere deep inside she felt the warming contentment of a raven's wings wrap slowly round her. Her words were barely audible. "It will be the sister who brings the willing heart and mind of a solitary witch to this place."

And with that, while the others simply saw a body on the bed before them, Idla flapped her great wings and took Veyanor on her final journey, eyes glinting as she assured the elderly witch all was well, and the Ancestors were already waiting.

The four witches looked from each to the other, knowing Veyanor had gone, far from happy none had been chosen from amongst them to take her place. Moments later, it had been agreed that no one else would ever hear of Veyanor's strange final request. Everything had to be kept secret. Together, they could surely find a way to bring the heart and mind of a solitary witch to the Meeting House.

They simply needed time and a plan.

A great Tzorkly Passing Ceremony was held on the smooth plateau of the Raising Stone a few days later, with witches and dignitaries from all fifteen Majickal Dales travelling to pay their respects. Feasting, drinking, singing, laughter, music and dance rang out over the entire torch lit valley. Never had so many witches and dales-creatures gathered together in the same place.

Afterwards, as the revelry continued in The Vroffa Tree Inn, the four coven leaders discreetly headed to a small upstairs room with a jug of Grimwagel Wine, telling Laffrohn they were not to be disturbed.

"I dare say you'll be sorting out the new Tzorkly High Priestess," the landlady said. "There's folk already saying that it be odd none has been chosen. Sooner it be resolved the better, methinks."

Bethgella narrowed her eyes. "Such matters are for the sisterhood, not innkeepers. Leave us be, if you don't want to feel the sting of our wands."

After Laffrohn left, the four filled their goblets and discussed their dilemma. However much they disliked hearing her words, the landlady was right – witches were wondering what would happen next. Once the celebrating stopped and the splurked heads cleared, everyone would want to know who was to be the new GrandTzorkly High Priestess.

"What we need," Bethgella said confidentially, "is someone we can make Grand Tzorkly High Priestess for a short time whilst we sort out the problem between us. We find ourselves a complete splurk, an utter no-hoper, make her leader, then stroff her once we can bring the heart and mind of a solitary witch to the Meeting Place."

The others considered this, Teghart nodding along appreciatively. "No one else was in the room when Veyanor stroffed. No one else heard her last request. We can say she decreed anything. Who's to know otherwise?"

Pruttel, leader of the Crooked Hats, agreed. "A fine plan. But who do we choose? And who has to stroff her, afterwards?"

Alfloria, of the Earth Weavers, had a suggestion. "I do know of one such witch who may be suitable." The others all leant forwards. "A most splurked Weaver, one I've always had my doubts about."

"And you'd also be prepared to stroff her when the time came?" Bethgella pressed.

Alfroria frowned. "I've offered the witch, that's enough. Someone else can stroff her."

"What's her name?"

"Sinchkin," Alforia replied. "I can speak to her in the morn'up."

SINCHKIN

The Spuddle of Sinchkin

If there was one thing other Earth Weavers knew about Sinchkin, it was that it would be very unlikely that the fiercely independent witch could be found *anywhere* on any given morning. Granted, she had a small and rather modest burrow, but even a casual visitor would know its owner didn't use it very often. For Sinchkin, home was wherever she chose to lay her small witches' hat; on her head under a twinkling night sky, by her side in a dripping cavern, or as a pillow, high in the treetops of a vast forest. She was a traveller, a wanderer, and enjoyed nothing more than seeing as much of the Majickal Dales as she could; the small villages, towns bustling with every description of creature, sweeping dales stretching as far as she could see – always wondering just what lay on the other side, and hoping she'd find out the very next day.

In her years, she'd travelled to all fifteen dales, yet knew in her heart she'd never see enough. Other places, creatures, majickal mysteries and saztaculous sights would always elude her. Yet she'd resolved this wouldn't be for lack of effort on her part.

When she did return from her trips, other Earth Weavers would gather in her burrow to hear fantastic tales of the places she'd visited. Some would sit agog, open mouthed in wonderment. Others would shake their heads insisting no good would come from such splurked adventures.

"But we are all sisters of the earth, mountains, forests, valleys, rivers and lakes," she'd explain to them. "We keep the secrets of such places. Not to see them, feel them, touch them, taste them, smell them, is to miss their most powerful majick."

And then someone would ask for a demonstration of what she'd learnt, or demand she concoct a new potion from plants taken on her travels. But Sinchkin would always refuse. At coven gatherings and feasts, she would entertain fellow Earth Weavers twice her age with tales of her adventures, standing on tables, amazing them with her discoveries. At the end, she'd always ask her enthralled audience if any would care to venture with her on her next travels, but all would politely decline, preferring instead to hear, rather than experience the majickal worlds beyond their homelands. Which suited Sinchkin fine. She bore no grudges, and even understood their need to stay rooted. It simply didn't work for her.

No one ever knew when she'd return. Sometimes she'd be back in just a moon-turn, other times her burrow could be empty for six whole seasons. And yet in those times, if anyone had bothered to venture inside and really look closely, they'd have made their own quite extraordinary discovery. For right at the back, beyond her modest bedchamber was a long, curving passage that opened onto another, much larger room full of precisely drawn maps of her travels. For Sinchkin was as much a chronicler as an adventurer. Alongside her many parchment maps were volumes of books of the different plants and creature species she'd encountered. One entire wall was covered with maps stitched together to make one of the most comprehensive studies of all fifteen Majickal Dales ever undertaken. The 'words' such as they were, were little more than symbols, each carefully arranged around the drawn centrepiece, making the entire room quite the most breath-taking study – and known to only Sinchkin alone. For most, she was either an irresponsible, loud-mouthed, unreliable adventurer – or a true heroine, finding new lands and the best entertainment at any gathering. But if any had truly got to know the plucky little witch, they'd have found quite the most fastidious and intelligent soul they'd come across.

Yet for all her many travels, there was one majickal place that had always eluded her – Trefflepugga Path. She'd first heard of the mysterious, ever moving series of valleys, woods and rivers many years previously on a visit to Sveag Dale, a four-day journey by broom and foot over the tallest mountain ranges. There, in the safety of the town, warming herself by a large tavern fire, she'd met slow-jarrocks for the first time. These large, cumbersome bearlike creatures were phenomenal guzzwort drinkers, and as the evening wore on, gradually took the little witch into their confidence.

"You can't be calling yourself any kind of an adventurer until you've set foot along Trefflepugga Path," one told her. He pointed at her with his razor-sharp claws. "And I'll tell you this. I may be the bravest jarrock from round these parts, but there be no way I'd be trying my luck on it."

"How do I find it?" Sinchkin asked, immediately curious. This curious path seemed too good to resist.

The jarrock merely laughed. "You don't," he said, downing his guzzwort. "It finds you."

"How so?"

"If I knew how it was that a path can have a mind of its own, I'd be the richest jarrock in the Majickal Dales."

On another of her travels, she met a Lid Sister who claimed she'd once flown over the path, amazed to see the land underneath changing and twisting before her eyes. "It's said that no witch can ever land on Trefflepugga Path," she'd told Sinchkin. "And those that have been so foolish to try have instantly stroffed. For the path is merely for dales-creatures to venture along, and then only those it itself has chosen. Some of them never return, lost forever, doomed to wander and starve, eventually stroffing from the many tricks of the path. Some creatures say that it's the oldest part of the dales. Spuddles tell of Trefflepugga Path being the very beating heart of all that's majickal. But 'tis well to be aware, for it has a cruelty, too, a wickedness. And none of our tzorkly kind has ever been offered the chance to journey along it, which is just as well, for the blinksnap that we set one foot to the ground, we'd be consumed by fire."

Now, if all this sounds rather off-putting, and the sort of place to leave well alone (especially if you were a witch) it's also worth remembering that for Sinchkin, the worse the warnings and spuddles became, the more she wanted to experience the peculiar majick of Trefflepugga Path for herself. It intrigued her beyond all measure, occupied her waking thoughts and lurked in the back of her darkest dreams. Yet no matter how far she'd journeyed, how far she'd flown on her small broom, she'd never once caught sight of it. Inevitably, this simply made her more determined. To find the elusive path and record its movements would surely be the greatest ever discovery for any tzorkly adventurer.

So it was that a week before Veyanor passed to the Ancients, Sinchkin had once again packed her small bag with provisions and set off on her broom high into the sky to resume her search for Trefflepugga Path – ensuring she was far away from her burrow when Alfloria and her large entourage arrived with news of her ascension to Grand Tzorkly High Priestess named by Veyanor herself on her deathbed with her final breath. However, in front of the empty burrow, Alfloria's face dropped.

Another Earth Weaver, Sinchkin's nearest neighbour, stepped forwards. "She took to the twinkling-lid a while back."

Alfloria sighed. "On another of her splurked adventures, I suppose?"

The witch nodded.

"And, of course, know one knows where's she's gone, or when she's going to be back?"

The witch shook her head.

"Grodelshammen!" Alfloria cursed. "The whole league is hearing of Veyanor's last wishes, and now Sinchkin is nowhere to be found?"

"With respect," the witch cautiously tried, "I'm not sure it would have made any difference. She's always been more of an adventurer than tzorkly leader."

Alfloria narrowed her eyes. "Listen very carefully, you splurk. Sinchkin has been chosen, and Sinchkin it will be. Now spread the word – we have to find her as soon as possible!"

Completely oblivious to the intense search, Sinchkin was determined to make one final journey to find Trefflepugga Path, no matter how long it took. Even the thought of five years was fine. She'd never been away as long, but then again, the prize had never been greater. To finally find and map the path would be her crowning glory. It didn't matter if a single soul never saw her maps, drawings and notes, or if no one believed her stories, *she* would know, and that would be enough.

Sometimes, she worried about the risks, but nothing truly majickal had ever been achieved or discovered without them. Besides, she told herself, there were risks everywhere, and if she were to stroff on a most magnificent quest, surely it was better than living in a boring burrow for her remaining years. The dangers of the path just drew her even more.

She began by flying north, away from her homelands, far out over Winchett Dale, Hoff Dale, Alfisc Dale and Sveag Dale. She was searching for the coast of the northernmost tip of the Majickal Dales, where the land met the chilled waters of The Icy Seas. From there, she resolved to journey east on foot along the many coastal pathways leading to Kipps Dale and Seevius Dale, before heading back west through the mountains of Calvert Dale and Ayrius Dale. She'd planned the route quite thoroughly, taking sections of maps and relevant notebooks from previous expeditions. But whereas those trips had been to explore the boundaries between dales, this time she wanted to explore each in turn, stopping in the darkest forests, investigating the deepest caves, travelling the wildest rivers. If Trefflepugga Path was real, Sinchkin was determined that this time she'd find it.

Most times on her travels she'd meet up with a dales-creature who might tag along for a few days. Whilst initially glad of the company (such encounters frequently yielded valuable local information) all too often they became rather irritating, and she was left stuck thinking of ways of sending them on their way without causing too much offence. She supposed that for dales-creature she represented a peculiar novelty, a lone witch out exploring with no real agenda other than to record her discoveries. And perhaps this was true. Most of the dales-creatures were fairly harmless, keen to show her things they thought she'd be interested in, endlessly curious about her lifestyle. Yet for all the many things she'd been shown, all the boring conversations she'd been forced to endure, she'd learned precious little about Trefflepugga Path. So on this journey, she'd determined not to be distracted by dales-creatures, as really, they most likely wouldn't be able to offer anything relevant, anyway.

And yet, of course, the moment she'd decided, fate showed its curious hand. Or in this case, the long black wing of a raven in a small witch's hat...

The search for Sinchkin had consumed thousands of witches. Rewards had been offered. Groups of Lid Sisters, Bindnaps, Crooked Hats and Earth Weavers scoured the lands for the elusive explorer. A whole moon-turn passed before Bethgella, Alfloria, Pruttel and Teghart met once again in secret, this time in a discreet upstairs room of the large Meeting House to discuss the dilemma.

"The longer this goes on, the more splurked it becomes," Teghart moaned, pouring herself a large tankard of Grimwagel wine. She pointed her short, stubby finger at Alfloria. "She's one of yours, you have to find her."

Alfloria gave a thin-lipped smile. "Because for all your Bindnap tools and knowledge, you're quite incapable of finding her, either?"

Teghart angrily slammed down her tankard. "You lead us to believe finding this little splurk would be easy!"

Bethgella felt the need to assert her elegant authority. "Nothing will be achieved by squabbling. The search continues. We simply offer more rewards. Someone will find her soon. We'll make her Grand Tzorkly High Priestess then move on with our own plans."

After the meeting ended, Pruttel pulled Teghart to one side, confidentially tipping her crooked hat and lowering her voice to a whisper. "I may have something interesting."

"Interesting?" Teghart replied, watching Alfloria and Bethgella take to their brooms and roar away.

"I found a solitary," Pruttel continued, her vloice barely above a whisper. "Tracked her to her hovel. No one else knows."

"And?"

"Why waste time looking for the Earth Weaver, when all we really needed was the heart and mind of a solitary witch?"

Teghart considered this, checking they were really alone. "The solitary is still in her hovel?"

Pruttel nodded. "She never leaves, too twizzled by the search for Sinchkin."

Teghart slowly clicked her long tongue across her sharp teeth. "Veyanor told us the next Tzorkly Hight Priestess would be the one who bought the willing heart and mind of a solitary witch to this place."

"Problem is, I doubt this one would be terribly willing."

Teghart reached into her tool belt and took out a thin curved knife, its glinting edge wickedly sharp. "Then we stroff her. Cut out her heart, crush her skull, remove her brains, bring them here."

Pruttel swallowed hard, nervously eyeing the blade, trying her best to be diplomatic. "It still doesn't make her 'willing' does it?"

Teghart simply smiled. "But what you have to realise is that if she's stroffed, she's hardly unwilling either, is she? Therefore, she must be " She waited, watching Pruttel struggle to follow the logic.

"Willing?"

"Exactly," Teghart beamed.

"It all seems most splurked."

"But absolutely accurate and true."

"Perhaps," Pruttel slowly admitted.

"And afterwards you and I can become joint Grand Tzorkly High Priestesses and rule together. How can we ever trust the other two? Alfloria can't even find a witch in her own coven, and Bethgella looks down on all three of us." She seized Pruttel by the shoulders. "Now is our chance to do this without them."

Silently wondering if she'd done the right thing, Pruttel reluctantly agreed, the two of them taking to their brooms to find the solitary witch.

"I know you're following me. Why don't you show yourself?" Sinchkin announced as she headed deeper into the forest. It was her third day in and amongst the giant trees. She'd first spotted the beginnings of the thick woodlands from the coastal pathway, stopping to check her maps and realising she hadn't noticed the small valley on her previous visits. Intrigued, she'd headed into the cool gloom, stopping to make notes about the various abundant mosses and shrooms carpeting the rich, peaty floor. The deeper she went, the larger the trees became, and with it something rather unusual   virtual silence. No creature scrittled amongst the fallen leaves, nothing crawled through the undergrowth, not a single birdcall came from above.

On her first night she slept soundly, waking in the early morning chill to the smoking embers of her dying campfire. She added dried twigs and leaves to revive the flames and made herself a brottle-leaf brew in her small hanging cauldron, still keenly aware of the silence.

Twice, it made her shudder, and she wondered whether to turn back, a thought quickly quashed by her urge to continue. After all, with no apparent predators, what harm could possibly befall her? Packing up, she put out the fire and set off, wand at the ready, just in case.

It was towards the end of the day that she first heard the rustling. She peered into the dense maze of trunks and branches, prepared to send a stinging vroosher at whoever – or whatever – was causing it. But nothing happened. Telling herself it was most likely a falling branch, she continued threading her way through the trees, trying as best as possible to use the rays of the setting sun as her guide.

When she finally made camp in a small clearing, she heard the noise a second time. Whatever it was, it was clearly following her. That night, she slept with her wand by her side.

The next day, the creature appeared to be getting bolder. At times she wondered if it was more than just one, and she was being hunted by a pack. However, as far as she could tell, most noises came from above her head, or occasionally on the ground, a familiar 'chik-chik-chik' accompanying them of a bird scrittling though the leaves.

It was time, she decided, to confront whatever it was. Wand at the ready, she called out into the trees. "I know you're following me. Why don't you show yourself?"

For a long time there was simply the pressing silence, Sinchkin's ears straining to hear above her own shallow breathing. "I mean you no harm. I have a little food, some water if you're thirsty."

This time she jumped as a sudden thrashing overhead revealed a large black bird flying straight into the clearing to land and look right at her. It had to be one of the biggest birds she'd ever seen, a good head taller than her with a long, dangerous beak. Trying not to look too twizzled, she took out some shrooms she'd gathered and scattered them on the ground, watching the bird listlessly peck at them, drawn by the witches' hat on its rather elegant head. "I have completely no idea what you are," she quietly said. "But you're welcome to what I have."

The bird looked at her with piercing black eyes, before suddenly shaking itself, outstretching its wings and literally shrinking before her eyes. Sinchkin had never seen anything like it before in all her life and many adventures. One moment it was looking down at her, the next had shrunk to a quarter of its original size.

Before she could even gasp in surprise it had risen from the ground and landed on her shoulder. She yelped, certain it would attack, yet the more she tried to twist and turn away, the harder the long talons dug in. Eventually, she gave up struggling, realising the calmer she was, the less the bird painfully gripped her. For a full two minutes, she simply stood in the clearing trying to compose herself, making an elaborate gesture of slowly putting away her wand.

"Well," she said quietly, horribly aware of the razor sharp beak just inches from her face. "Whoever you are, it seems you're here to stay." She looked around. "I'm supposing you live here, and as you seem to be very much in charge, which way do you suggest we go now?"

The bird's talons gripped a little harder, its beak pointing through the trees ahead.

"This way? Why not? Let's give it a try."

So it was that Sinchkin spent the rest of the day being guided through the forest by Idla, without ever realising the tzorkly significance of the moment. Other Earth Weavers might have recognised the great, majickal raven from spuddles they'd once heard, but for Sinchkin, such legends were far too splurked to be even vaguely believable. Even those she'd once been told she'd largely forgotten. What was the point in such stories from the past, as useless to an explorer as a torn map. Sinchkin's world was one of *real* majick, real places, real things. To have even entertained the thought that she now walked with a mythical bird as her guide would have been completely laughable. And yet its hat did intrigue her...

"I presume you stole it from an unfortunate witch," she said, pointing up at the brim. "Your kind often takes things. But you do wear it well, I have to say."

The bird leant down and looked at her in the eye. *'What you 'presume', and what actually happens, are entirely misinformed by your own ambitions.'*

Sinchkin's jaw dropped. "You can speak?"

'Apparently.'

"But your beak didn't move."

'Something new for your notebooks, perhaps?'

Her eyes widened. "You did it again! I can hear you, but you're not saying anything."

'Maddening, isn't it?'

"What are you? Who are you?"

'A messenger.'

Sinchkin tried to heave the bird from her shoulder, crying out as the long long talons dug back in.

'We can do this all day – or we can go where I tell you to.'

"Just leave me alone!"

'Frankly, with your attitude, I'd rather like to. But I answer to the Ancients, not you. And besides, the moment I left you, you'd burst into flames and burn.'

It took a few moments for the revelation to sink in, Sinchkin slowly piecing together what she already knew about the place she sought. She took a deep breath, her hesitant voice barely above a whisper. "Because no witch can survive on Trefflepugga Path?"

The bird stretched out a long black wing and pointed to a large oak up ahead. *'Watch.'*

Sinchkin sucked in a breath as almost imperceptibly, the tree began to move. Then others around it, inch by inch, slowly separating and pulling sideways to form a pathway into the darkest reaches of the forest beyond. "It's true," she whispered, heart pounding. "It exists."

'Right now," Idla told her, *'there are many witches looking for you. Great rewards have been placed for your capture. You are in danger. My duty is to protect and take you somewhere no witch would ever find you – or stroff, if they tried.'*

But Sinchkin wasn't listening. Nothing mattered to her outside this one majickal moment. All her life she'd looked, but somehow, some way, she'd finally found an entrance to Trefflepugga Path.

Or, perhaps, it had found her.

Stroffing a witch is a grisly business – and as such best avoided as much as possible. There are (unfortunately for the witches concerned) several options, all of them involving considerable pain and intense heat. The first and most reliable method is by way of a wand. Charge your wand by repeatedly shaking it. When the end frizzes bright blue, send a white-hot, stinging vroosher straight into your target. A close enough strike should accomplish the deed more or less instantly. However, a word of caution for the novice wand user – always strike from behind. If your intended victim gets the merest hint of your intentions, she'll most likely turn, draw, charge and loose her wand far faster than you could ever imagine.

Boiling is another method, although for this you need a group of brave and willing accomplices to first capture and bind your witch, together with a large enough cauldron to complete the task. Smaller cauldrons can be used, but only if the witch can be forced in headfirst – a tricky, messy and dangerous business.

Other methods include tricking witches into swallowing hot rocks, the use of heated spears, molten lead, and even slow-roasting over an open fire – but these should only really be used by the most experienced witch, as the preparation and skill required can be truly rather arduous.

The most trusted method is unsurprisingly, plain and simple fire – especially useful if it's a sleeping solitary witch who thinks herself safe in her hovel. Constructed from branches, animal pelts and dried leaves, hovels are dangerously ready-made for the purpose, as Teghart discovered when Pruttel lead her to her secret discovery later that night.

"You're sure she's still in there?" Teghart asked, taking out her wand and licking her lips.

Pruttel nodded, anxiously looking round. The small valley clearing seemed deserted, the only noise the slow bubbling of a brook running contentedly under the clear moonlight. She watched Teghart take aim, wondering just how wise it had been to make a deal with her. What 'bind' would Teghart place her in? Could she really be trusted to share being Grand Tzorkly High Priestess? Bindnapps were as famous for their cunning as their making skills – just how splurked had she been to lead Teghart to this place?

"Ready?" Teghart asked.

Pruttel nodded and took out her own wand, the blue tip already frizzing as she levelled it at the hovel.

"Now!"

The vrooshers shot out, and in moments it was ablaze. Flames shot from the small hovel as a screaming witch emerged, clothes already on fire. Pruttel and Teghart swiftly loosed again, sending fatal vrooshers no witch could ever withstand, before dragging the smouldering body into the brook to douse the last of the flames and laying it back out on the bank, their breath coming in short gasps.

"Well," Teghart managed to say, taking out her long knife. "After that, I suspect the rest is going to be thankfully much easier."

Pruttel simply stood in shock, rooted to the spot, as if struggling to absorb what had happened.

"You were just a part of this as I was," Teghart reminded her. "No one forced your wand."

"That was the most splurked thing I ever saw," she quietly said.

"Well, it's just about to get a lot worse," Teghart replied, holding the point of the knife against the dead witch's chest. "But those that wish to wield the wand of power must also be prepared to wield the knife." She looked Pruttel directly in the eye. "Do I sense hesitation from you?"

Pruttel swallowed.

"Because, sister, if that be the case, then maybe power isn't something you are ready for. Some never are. T'would be a most glopped shame if you were one of them."

Pruttel set her face, quickly snatching the knife from Teghart's hand. "I'm ready. More than ready. I'll do the heart, you do the brains."

A few minutes later they were done, the bloody heart and brains of the solitary witch safely in a cloth bag, the remains tossed back into the last of the burning hovel. Satisfied, Teghart cleaned her knife in the brook before the two of them set back off on their brooms to the Great Meeting Hall, whooping with delight as they passed under the twinkling night sky.

At the hall, they dismounted, taking the wretched bag inside, Teghart immediately sitting on the large throne, smiling as she and ran her hands along the carved wooden armrests. "Well," she calmly observed. "The strange thing is that however hard I look, I just can't see two thrones."

"What do you mean?" Pruttel slowly replied, eyes slowly narrowing.

Teghart chuckled. "I'm thinking perhaps we're one too many for the job." She saw Pruttel's hands twitch towards her wand, instantly drawing her own and aiming across the hall.

"Surely you wouldn't stroff me?" Pruttel squealed, fumbling and dropping her own wand. "The others would know you did it! How would you explain it?"

Teghart pretended to look confused, then suddenly burst out laughing. "Because I'll stroff them, too, you splurk! And the Earth Weaver when they find her. Then who would dare question me when I have the throne?"

"Teghart, I'm begging you..."

"I know," Teghart sighed, flicking her wrist and sending a bright blue vroosher straight through Pruttel's chest, savouring the look of shock on her dying face. "And it was very polite of you. But simply not enough, I'm afraid." She flicked her wrist once more, watching Pruttel fall heavily onto the stone floor.

Without wasting a moment on sentiment, she opened the cloth bag and placed the heart and brains on each arm of the throne. "Ancient sisters!" she cried, looking up into the ornately carved roof. "Veyanor herself declared the next Grand Tzorkly High Priestess would be the one who bought the willing heart and mind of a solitary witch to this place. I have bought both, and as they are clearly not *unwilling*, I have therefore fulfilled her tzorkly conditions and duly declare myself rightful Grand Tzorkly High Priestess of *The League of Lid-Curv*..."

She stopped, twizzled as the great room had began to fill with swirling, translucent figures in robes and witches hats. They began to chant, Teghart's eyes widening as she saw Pruttel's abandoned wand slowly rise from the floor, tip already frizzing as it glided menacingly towards her. "No!" she begged. "Please! I've done everything you asked!"

But the Ancients disagreed, speeding their chant as Teghart suddenly bolted from the throne, the wand following before it vrooshed and stroffed her right next to Pruttel.

Moments later, the hall fell silent once more.

By nature, Sinchkin was nothing if not adaptable, and if the price for exploring this most curious and majickal of places was merely to have a talking raven on her shoulder, then so be it. Granted, Idla's weight sometimes became uncomfortable, but even the bird seemed to be able to sense just when to switch shoulders, or even perch on her head when Sinchkin removed her hat. The long talons, though, were still sharp, but the ever resourceful witch managed to soften their impact by placing rounded bark on her shoulders, tying it under her arms with reeds for Idla to perch on.

'*We must look quite a sight,*' Idla silently observed, her words now freely accepted visitors in Sinchkin's mind.

"It's not us I'm looking at," Sinchkin replied, taking out her notebook and trying to sketch a distant mountain that seemed to move faster than a witch in flight. She cursed, closing the book, the drawing just a bad blur. "It's useless. Nothing ever stays still. Not for the oidiest blinksnap."

'*It's Trefflepugga Path. What else did you expect? To map it? It would be like trying to stop water running through your fingers.*'

As if to prove the point, the ground before them suddenly moved, splitting to reveal a small stream rising up in the gap, twisting and writhing like a snake.

Sinchkin sighed. "I just want to understand it. After all, why am I here, if not to make sense of it?"

Once again, Idla explained the search to find and make her Tzorkly High Priestess.

And once again, Sinchkin barely listened.

'*What is it that irks you so about the league?*'

"Irks me? Nothing irks me."

'*Then leave here, be found, become Grand Tzorkly High Priestess. It's a position of great honour.*'

Sinchkin sat on the rich mossy grass, watching the landscape slowly changing before her eyes, feeling it undulate, almost breathe beneath her.

Idla climbed down onto her lap. *This path was the beginning of everything, the very heartbeat and lifeblood of all that's truly majickal. It was here many moon-turns before any dales-creature or witch. Some say it was the path itself that created all life, others that it was Oramus, an all-seeing being who lives in the moon. But whatever the truth, few can deny that Trefflepugga Path is alive. It has whims, desires, a destiny beyond anything we could ever imagine. It only ever calls certain creatures to journey along it, and they only go where it decides. Many stroff here for reasons it alone knows. Others are given safe passage. Some of the best creatures never return, while the worst live on, unharmed. But whatever its motives, it also brings such sheer majickal beauty. Sometimes I think to stroff here might not be such a splurked thing.*

Sinchkin watched as an entire forest seemed to climb a large mountainside, thousands of trees rising from the ground heading for the the summit. "Is this where you stroffed?"

My calling has no relevance. I serve a Higher Purpose, now.

"Because you want to, or the path made you?"

There was a long silence.

Each moment, every blinksnap, is always complete in itself. Your maps tell us nothing of the now, simply how the land was. Yet each action is dependant on both a past and a future that, if we really looked and tried to understand, shape us equally.

Sinchkin frowned. "I think you've been eating too many bad shrooms, bird. They can play splurked games with your head."

Idla softly chuckled. *Yet here you are, talking to a raven that never opens its beak.*

Sinchkin smiled, yawning, lying down, suddenly very tired. "Can I sleep here? Or will I burst into flames in the middle of the night?"

Idla settled on her chest. *As long as I'm with you, you'll be safe.*

"Thank you."

It's simply my calling.

"One thing, though, can we have less of the splurked conversations about moments and futures? They're really terribly dull."

Idla clicked her throat, the first audible noise she'd made, leaving Sinchkin wondering if the peculiar raven was either tired, or simply laughing at her.

"You've heard about the other two?" Bethgella asked, as she and Alfloria sat in the meeting hall of the Lid Sister's coven.

"I never trusted either of them," Alfloria replied.

Bethgella smiled. "Apparently, the solitary's heart and brains were still on the arms of the throne."

Alfloria shuddered. "Savages."

"Completely," Bethgella agreed. "But for me, it does raise an interesting question."

"How so?"

"All this distrust, so distressing, and yet it also makes me wonder just how trustworthy *you* are, Alfloria."

"Me?"

Bethgella pointed a long finger. "You said finding your Earth Weaver would be easy. Yet there's been no trace of her. Everyone thinks she is our next Grand Tzorkly High Priestess and wants to know where she is. The whole situation is completely splurked. We made the announcement and now look like fools. It's been bad enough trying to keep the deaths of Teghart and Pruttel quiet. If the Crooked Hats and Bindnaps discover the truth, there'll be a war."

Alfloria watched as Bethgella paced the hall. "But that was their doing, not mine. They stroffed the solitary. Not me. I've stayed loyal by your side."

Bethgella slowly turned. "But how do I know you don't know *precisely* where your elusive little Earth Weaver actually is right now? How do I know you've not sent everyone on a hunt to find someone you're already hiding?"

"That's the most splurked thing you've ever said!"

"Is it?" Bethgella hissed, levelling her wand at Alfloria's head. "I daresay you've got this whole thing planned. First, you stroff Teghart and Pruttel. Next, it's me. Then you suddenly 'find' your Earth Weaver and arrange a splurked 'accident' when she's Grand Tzorkly High

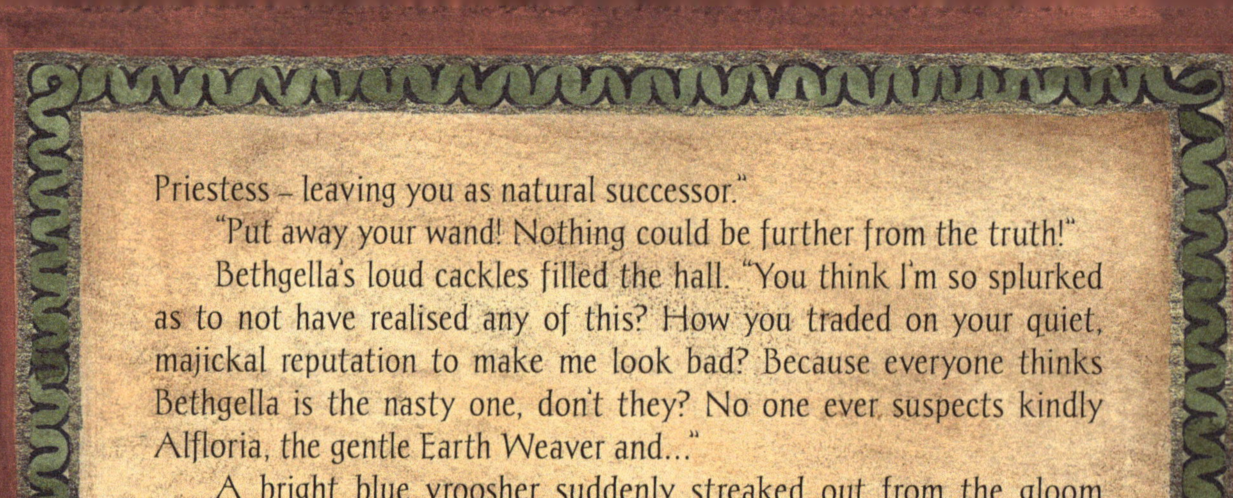

Priestess – leaving you as natural successor."

"Put away your wand! Nothing could be further from the truth!"

Bethgella's loud cackles filled the hall. "You think I'm so splurked as to not have realised any of this? How you traded on your quiet, majickal reputation to make me look bad? Because everyone thinks Bethgella is the nasty one, don't they? No one ever suspects kindly Alfloria, the gentle Earth Weaver and…"

A bright blue vroosher suddenly streaked out from the gloom knocking Bethgella's wand from her hand.

"What is this?" she cried, as Lid Sisters began slowly emerging from their hiding places, wands levelled.

Alfloria smiled. "You lost your coven the moment you lost the race to the Raising Stone, Bethgella. The leader of the Lid Sisters, humbled and beaten by a simple splurk from Trasgar? You became the laughing stock of the dales – only you always had your head too far in the clouds to ever realise."

The Lid Sisters surrounded their leader, wand tips frizzing.

"Alfloria!" Bethgella ordered. "Call them off."

"Oh, but I made a deal," Alfloria laughed. "The age of *The League of Lid-Curving Witchery* is over. Veyanor's pathetic attempts to unite the four covens will soon lie in ruins. You're right – a war is coming. Bindnaps will rise against Crooked Hats to avenge their dead leaders. Lid Sisters and Earth Weavers will combine to form one brand new coven – Lid Weavers. Sisters of both the air and the ground. As above, so below. And all talk of being 'tzorkly' will stroff as surely as the league itself."

Bethgella slowly shut her eyes, shaking her head, wondering how it was she had missed the obvious. "With you as leader, I suppose?"

Alfloria nodded. "Your Lid Sisters agreed, as did my Earth Weavers."

Bethgella looked at the ring of frizzing wands surrounding her. "But tell me one final thing – where have you hidden your little splurk?"

"Sinchkin?" Alfloria laughed, "I haven't. I have absolutely no idea where she is. Which makes it so much easier for me to seize my opportunity. Goodbye, Bethgella."

Moments later, the wands hit their mark.

When Sinchkin woke, it was still night. She knew it *should* be morning as she had slept soundly and felt completely refreshed, yet overhead stars still twinkled and a full moon lit the valley that had crept up and surrounded her as she'd slept.

'It can be confusing at first.'

She raised herself up onto an elbow, Idla shifting and climbing up onto her shoulder as she slowly stood. "So I gather."

'Day and night have no meaning on Trefflepugga Path. Neither does time itself. Here you can be stuck for a lifetime, only to emerge a mere blinksnap before you ventured in.'

Sinchkin was in no mood for riddles. Her shoulder still ached from the weight of the annoying bird, and despite her asking it not to, it was still talking complete nonsense. Day or night, to her this was morning and she needed some breakfast.

She set off along the narrow valley, moonlight illuminating the slowly moving mountains. When the path looked as if it would veer left, it turned right. When she thought it climbed, the ground shifted and descended, valley sides narrowing as she looked for succulent shoots or shrooms she could eat.

Yet after a while, the path began to level, giving way to flatter grasses and just a few scattered trees. In the distance a fire crackled sending long flicking shadows across the valley. Her ears pricked as she heard voices, and made out the unmistakeable shape of a large steaming cauldron under an old tree. Instantly she drew her small wand.

'You're majick is useless on the path,' Idla scolded her. *'What oidy wand could ever match it?'*

Peering ahead, Sinchkin made out two witches stirring the cauldron, moonlight glinting off the long ladle. One held a glowing vroffa-broom, while the other's red hair danced in the breeze.

'You are here,' Idla said. *'The rest is up to you. Approach the cauldron. Stand on the small rock next to it. You will be safe – for now.'*

Sinchkin yelped as Idla launched herself from her shoulder and flew up into the tree. Instantly the ground beneath her small feet began to glow bright red. The heat was intolerable. Crying out, she scrambled for the small rock, clambering up, the pain thankfully receding.

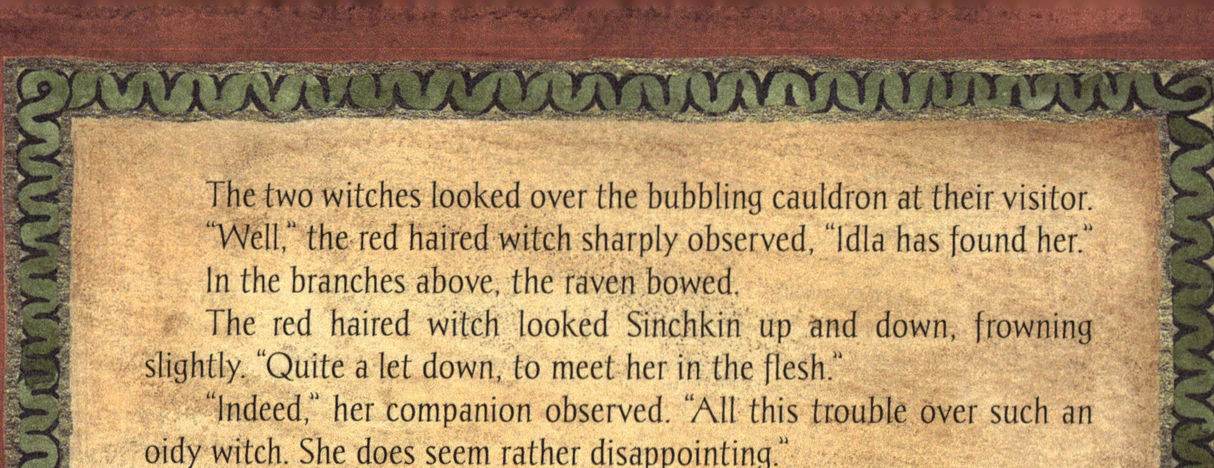

The two witches looked over the bubbling cauldron at their visitor.

"Well," the red haired witch sharply observed, "Idla has found her."

In the branches above, the raven bowed.

The red haired witch looked Sinchkin up and down, frowning slightly. "Quite a let down, to meet her in the flesh."

"Indeed," her companion observed. "All this trouble over such an oidy witch. She does seem rather disappointing."

"And yet the path and the Ancients have willed it, which also cannot be denied. Our feelings about her suitability for such a majickal task are made irrelevant. The motives are quite hidden from us, as they always have been," the red haired witch sighed. She pointed at Sinchkin. "Yet it all seems so splurked. Why look, she barely rises to my knee."

"Oidy she may be," the other witch agreed, "yet she also shows no twizzles, either. There's many who might stand in her place right now who would be shaking so badly they'd have quite fallen from the only rock that keeps her from the fires."

The red haired witch looked at the small rock under Sinchkin's feet. "True," she admitted. "It does seem that the rock itself has been fashioned for the oidiest witch. I would have trouble balancing on it with just one leg."

"So perhaps this oidy explorer is indeed a destiny foretold." The second witch gently prodded Sinchkin in her heavily beating chest. "See? She stands quite rooted to it. As true as any that stood on the flattest ground."

"And yet, she says not a word."

"But challenges with her eyes. As if the very fires of Trefflepugga Path blaze within them. Such spirit in such an oidy thing." The second witch smiled at Sinchkin.. "Welcome, Sinchkin, eternal wanderer. You are finally home."

Sinchkin said nothing, trapped on the rock, wondering if she could possibly make a grab for the broom and fly away. Granted, it was huge compared to her own broom, but it would be better than being boiled for breakfast.

The second witch suddenly looked at her. "But why would you wish to fly away, Sinchkin?" Her voice was quieter, kinder than her red-haired companion. "Aren't you happy here on the path? Isn't it everything you ever desired – to discover Trefflepugga Path, then map its ever-twisting journey?"

Sinchkin tried not to sound too twizzled. "You are both large witches. I am just an Earth Weaver. You would need a witch four times my size to eat your fill."

The kinder witch laughed. "Don't you know who we are?"

"No. I simply want to be on my way with my bird."

The red-haired witch snarled, hissing through her long sharp teeth. "The soothwing does our bidding, not yours, you insolent splurk! Idla led you to us in the first place!" She took a breath, slightly shocked. "You really have no idea who we are?"

Sinchkin shook her head.

The kinder witch chuckled. "Then it is exactly as foretold." She leant down to Sinchkin. "Until recently, I was Grand Tzorkly High Priestess of The League of Lid-Curving Witchery. My name is Veyanor." She pointed at the frowning red-haired witch. "And this is Algorin, an explorer and adventurer just like you who made The Great Crossing from The Howling Lands and established Trasgar, first home of the league."

It was Sinckin's turn to frown. "You're both already stroffed?"

Veyanor nodded, lowering her voice to a whisper. "How else do you think we can survive on the path?" She pointed to the raven in the branches. "And that's Idla the Soothwing, messenger of the Ancients, who upon our bidding bought you to us."

"You really haven't heard of me?" Algorin asked, bemused. "Surely, I am the most famous of all the league's sisters?"

Sinchkin looked from one to the other. However splurked the situation was, she couldn't ignore the obvious dangers. The cauldron was still furiously boiling. It wouldn't take much for either of them to toss her straight into it. "I simply want to be on my way," she said. She looked at Algorin. "If it makes you feel any better, I do remember some spuddles about you."

Algroin expectantly raised her eyebrows. "And?

"And even if you both really are who you say you are, I can only speak my truth."

Veyanor chuckled. "For one so oidy, she has a big heart."

"Or a splurked head," Algorin replied. "Careful with your words, Sinchkin, for while I no longer require broth, it would still give me great pleasure to see the skin drop from your oidy bones."

Sinchkin steadied herself on the rock. "The spuddles I heard of Algorin told of a splurked witch who ran away from her sisters when they most needed her. A savage witch that took only the weakest on a journey to escape her own death and maintain her lust for power." She looked Algorin fearlessly in the eyes. "She was a witch who only cared for her own survival. Many were lost in The Icy Seas, yet she survived, only to be overpowered by the dales-creatures who built Trasgar all around her while she did nothing and witches were banished to their own quarter and treated as splurked amusements for rich merchant families."

Algorin sadly shook her head. "So much gets lost in the telling over time."

Veyanor pressed. "And me? What do you know of me?"

Sinchkin's gaze was rock steady. "Why do you wish to know? Why not just boil me and be done with it?"

"Because I've never boiled another witch and don't intend to start now."

"Fine, then let me on my way."

"Leave the rock and the path will stroff you. Answer my question – or leave and burn. The choice is yours."

Sinchkin looked at the ground surrounding the small rock. The thought of taking just the lightest step on it was truly twizzlyfying. "Fine," she told Veyanor. "Here's what I know of you. You bought vroffa-branches to the dales that only increased the Lid Sisters' dominion over the skies. You built a great meeting house that only you truly enjoyed. You lived a life convinced you'd united the four covens, but in reality did little for any of them. You claimed to have settled disputes, yet did so with no knowledge of the long history behind them. You proclaimed your judgements as final, yet you were nothing other than a broom-maker from Trasgar. How could you possibly believe anyone would really respect you as anything other than a self-appointed splurk whose only ambition was her own selfish vanity?"

There was a long silence before Algorin slowly began to chuckle. "And I thought mine was bad. Groydelshammen, Veyanor, your legacy is really splurked!"

"Nonsense," Veyanor snapped. "It's just the opinion of an oidy little Weaver!"

"But what if," Algorin teased, "she's right and we're wrong? What if that's how other witches really see us?"

Veyanor frowned. "Nonsense. We are two of the greatest witches." She looked at Sinchkin. "And the fates have decreed that you shall be the third."

Sinchkin began to laugh. " Me? You're splurked league means nothing to me."

"Do you know," Algorin asked her, "the true purpose of Trefflepugga Path?"

Sinchkin sighed. "Your bird tried to explain it. Frankly, it got incredibly dull."

"Then let me try," Algorin persisted. "It plays with your ambitions. You thought yours was to find it, but it found you. You wanted to map it, but how can you map what constantly moves? A thousand lifetimes wouldn't be enough. So now you are stuck, unable to leave a mere rock for the rest of your life. And the only person you can blame, Sinckin, is yourself. In the end, your own free spirit trapped you. Soon, Idla won't be here to guide you anymore. You will simply have what remains of your days to wonder how it all went so terribly wrong."

"You could leave me that broom," Sinchkin tried. "I could fly away."

Veyanor slowly shook her head. "Great unrest is coming. All trace of creature-witches will soon vanish forever from the Majickal Dales."

"It's true," Algorin added. "Every word. But there is another way, another possibility. The next Grand Tzorkly High Priestess will possess the willing heart and mind of a solitary witch. And whilst you are an Earth Weaver, you're also an explorer with a brave heart and bold ambitions. Whilst you profess little allegiance to The League of Lid

Curving Witchery, should you choose, you will be the one to truly unite all witches as the Ancients always intended."

"Or," Veyanor warned, "stay on your rock until the path claimes you."

"Both choices are splurked," Sinchkin sourly replied. "Either way, I stroff - here, or by the wands of the others. None would accept me as leader, and I have no ambition to be one."

"Then," Veyanor sighed, "our work here is done. We will leave the cauldron. The fire beneath will burn for a while. You could simply end the agony by throwing yourself in. It will be quicker than burning on the path. Goodbye, Sinchkin, and I hope life has given you all the answers you constantly sought."

She watched as both witches faded before her eyes, looking into the tree for Idla, seeing it too was empty. All that remained was a bubbling cauldron that began to look increasingly tempting as her tired legs began to wobble on the small rock.

Over the next few days, skirmishes broke out between Bindnaps and Crooked Hats as news of their coven leaders' deaths spread. Each coven blamed the other, all harmony destroyed as sisters sought out each other in increasingly deadly attacks. In and amongst the chaos, old feuds resurfaced, both covens turning not only on each other, but also themselves as the madness grew.

Watching and waiting, Alfloria and the Lid Sisters timed their moment, keeping themselves as far away from the troubles as they could.

"Soon," Alfloria told them, "we will attack the survivors by land and air. All Crooked Hats must be stroffed; they are of no use to anyone. Only save the best Bindnaps as our makers and builders. Those that refuse will boil."

The Lid Sisters agreed, glad to finally have a leader who commanded more respect than Bethgella ever had. Temporarily, at least. For in confidently making a pact with the untrustworthy, superior sisters of the sky, Alforia's caution had been crushed by her ambition. Her reign would be short lived, the Lid Sisters simply biding their time before choosing the moment to strike down Alfloria and her Earth Weavers to fully inherit both the skies and the earth below. None who survived would ever dare challenge the their permanent dominion again. The dales-creatures would learn to fear their new rulers, all thoughts of sharing the dales forgotten as easily as The League of Lid-Curving Witchery.

What started with The Great Crossing would end in great victory for the Lid Sisters. And it would shortly be theirs to seize...

Sinchkin woke with a start, instinctively clinging onto the branch, harsh sunlight in her eyes. Trying to focus, she gradually remembered events from the long night before: how she'd finally summoned the courage to leap from the rock, taking one step on the scorching ground before wrapping herself around the tree-trunk and scrambling up into the branches to safety and sleep.

How long she'd slept? It looked like early morning, but was it another trick of the path? Would the sun suddenly disappear to reveal a silvered moon rising in a night full of stars? She looked at the cauldron below, a final few wisps of smoke drifting from underneath. A thick brown liquid cooled inside. There'd be no way she could boil herself in there, even if she wanted to.

She laughed. The whole situation was utterly preposterous, completely absurd – and worse, totally unfair. What had she ever done to deserve it? Her whole life had simply been dedicated to exploring, wandering the dales to find new creatures, new places and recording her observations. Her obsession harmed no one, changed nothing for the worse. Yet, some-how, it had ended here, starving to death in the tree for fear of treading on the ground.

Trefflepugga Path, they'd warned her, would play with her ambitions. And it had. She was powerless to move, hopelessly stuck, alone and getting weaker by the blinksnap. But at least, she tried to console herself, it couldn't get any worse.

The path, however, had other ideas.

Clinging to the branch, she felt tiny vibrations ripple through her small hands as the tree's roots now gripped and dug themselves deeper into the soil, the entire tree gradually burying itself as the deadly ground rose up to meet her.

"Croydelshammen!" she cursed, desperately climbing higher as the tree descended, branches snapping under her grasp as she finally reached the very top.

She looked down, the trunk now completely buried, and saw her only twizzly option. Taking a deep breath, she yelled and leapt as far as she could, landing a blinksnap later in the cauldron, its luke-warm slurry covering her in foul gloop.

"This," she gasped, as the last of the tree disappeared into the ground behind her, "is going too far!" She balled her small fist up into the clear blue sky, years of rage and frustrating suddenly bursting out. "I have done nothing to deserve this!" She shook her head to try and clear swill from her ears. "And if you think I'm going to stroff in a cold cauldron on your splurked path, you're very wrong! How I stroff is my choice to make, not yours   and I would prefer to be free and running, even if I burn to death. So do your best, Trefflepugga Path, stroff me to ashes, but always know that I chose to do it, not you!"

Wiping her face and gripping her small wand, utterly determined to be the mistress of her own destiny, she let out one final yell and leapt from the cauldron onto the ground, eyes screwed tightly shut, waiting for the searing, burning pain to begin.

Nothing happened.

Taking short, twizzled breaths, she slowly opened her eyes and looked down. All around, the ground glowed its fiery red, and yet her feet felt as if they stood on the coolest grass, without the oidest bit of pain, whatsoever.

She took a few cautionary steps forward, still waiting for the flames to suddenly seize and bite.

Still nothing.

She looked back at the cauldron watching as it too sank into the hot ground, thick boiling gloop spilling and hissing over the sides until nothing remained.

Then she ran, faster than ever before, tears of relief streaming down her small face "I've done it!" she yelled. "I've beaten you, Trefflepugga Path! It was always my choice, not yours!"

But high up on the steep valley to her side, a sudden cracking bought a new and terrifying danger. Huge boulders now began tumbling down, demolishing trees, bouncing and smashing into each other, leaving vast craters as they hurtled towards her.

Twizzled, Sinchkin aimed her wand at the rocks and shot out a quick series of vrooshers that merely glanced off. The boulders thundered on, the sound filling the whole valley.

'Command them,' Idla's voice suddenly said. 'Command them as the witch of your destiny you now are. Not the Sinchkin you were, but the only witch who ever walked the path. Command and believe.'

She turned, frantically looking for the black raven, seeing nothing, the whole valley now a murderous avalanche. Steeling herself, with just moments to spare, she levelled her wand, crying at the top of her voice, "In the name of the Grand Tzorkly High Priestess of *The League of Lid-Curving Witchery*, I command you to stop!"

The rocks froze, as if caught in one of her drawings. One literally hung in the air, inches from the top of her hat.

She looked down at her wand, its tip still frizzing bright blue. "Idla? Are you there?"

'Do you need me to be – a mere splurked black bird?'

She tried to smile. "I only said that because I was twizzled."

'Has it occurred to you that I've always been here, if only you chose to ask? And that the Ancients have always been watching you?'

"I'm not so happy about that bit."

Idla's voice chuckled softly in her mind. *The path has shown you your true destiny, the power you really possess. Not to map things, but change them. The League of Lid-Curving Witchery needs a new Grand Tzorkly High Priestess to fearlessly challenge what seems impossible, to explore and map its bold new beginnings.'*

"But I know nothing of the league," Sinchkin insisted.

'And yet – you know everything. Now is your time to 'rise above' to be truly 'tzorkly'.'

Sinchkin watched as slowly the steep valley levelled into one vast sweeping dale. The large boulder above her head plopped gently onto the ground by her side, joining others as it rolled away into the distance. Above them, came a loud roar as a fire-trail split the clear blue sky and a huge dragon circled way overhead.

'Show no fear. She comes to you as she once came for Algorin. Your journey here is done.'

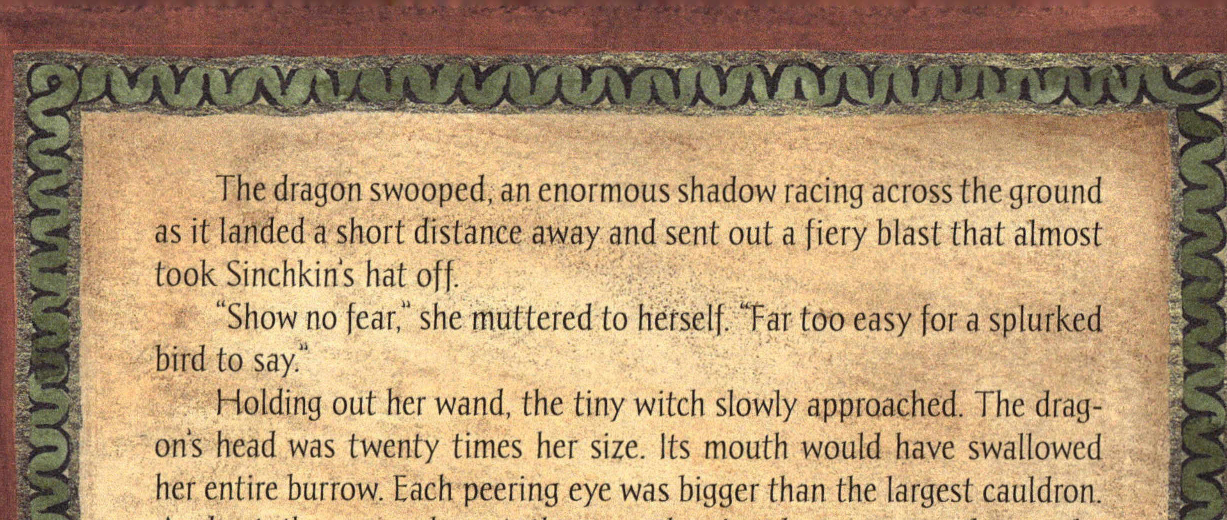

The dragon swooped, an enormous shadow racing across the ground as it landed a short distance away and sent out a fiery blast that almost took Sinchkin's hat off.

"Show no fear," she muttered to herself. "Far too easy for a splurked bird to say."

Holding out her wand, the tiny witch slowly approached. The dragon's head was twenty times her size. Its mouth would have swallowed her entire burrow. Each peering eye was bigger than the largest cauldron. And yet, the nearer she got, the more the giant beast appeared to settle, its breathing slowing and echoed around the dale.

When she was close enough, she looked up at the enormous head, a talon twice her size shifting in the earth by her feet. "My name's Sinchkin," she said. "I mean you no harm, and hope the same is true of you."

The dragon lowered its head.

"I wish," she went on, "to become tzorkly. I wish to become Grand Tzorkly High Priestess of *The League of Lid-Curving Witchery*."
The dragon simply looked at her, flicking its long barbed tail dangerously across the ground.

"But...but I don't know how, or what to do, or why." She took a breath, voice shaking. "But I would *really* love to ride on a dragon."

For a while the beast did nothing, simply staring at her, as if trying to make up its mind. Finally, after what seemed like an age, it offered its neck to climb on, the two of them taking to the sky, Sinchkin's excited cries ringing all round.

And as they flew, Trefflepugga Path followed, twisting and turning underneath like one vast snake, bending rivers, flattening mountains, creating vast gorges, dividing forests, gouging lakes, clinging to the dragon's beating shadow as together they crossed the Majickal Dales.

Far away in the remote western dale of Chilsopp, Alfloria, her Earth Weavers and the Lid Sisters watched from the shelter of the woodland as two great armies of Bindnaps and Crooked Hats gathered in the vast open plain before them. She estimated there must be over five thousand, most of their remaining number. Many had perished in previous battles, raids and skirmishes between the two covens. This was the day she would strike. When the final battle looked done, the Lid Sisters would take to their brooms, then her Earth Weavers rush from the forest to finish any survivors. After, there would be a great feast. The Lid Sisters would be made to raise their goblets to the famous victory, before gulping down the Grimwagel wine that she already had waiting for them in poisoned barrels. She had no need to share her glory with any other coven than her own. The Lid Sisters would be useful on this day, but nothing else besides. By morning, all would be dead. And then? There would simply be Earth Weavers, sole inheritors of the Majickal Dales. All opposition would have been eliminated. Everything would be theirs.

A great horn sounded, and the two armies of Bindnapps and Crooked Hats headed straight for each other. Hundreds of witches from both sides took to the air, streaking down lethal vrooshers at those below. Many fell from the sky to join the dead. Never had Alfloria seen such slaughter. She licked her lips at the eagerness her enemies willingly blamed and stroffed each other. Each dead witch was one less to worry about – another step closer to her final ambition.

"When do we attack?" a Lid Sister hissed, keen not to miss out.

"When they are nearly done," Alfloria smiled. "Why waste your precious vroffa, when they are so obliging at stroffing each other for us?"

The Lid Sister chuckled, enjoying the spectacle as three dead witches fell heavily to the ground just short of the treeline. One still clung to her broom, the end arrowed into the earth, the still-smoking body slowly falling off. "Needs to work on the landing, methinks."

"What's that?" A crouching Earth Weaver suddenly cried, pointing up at the sky.

Alfloria narrowed her eyes, peering through the trees as a great roaring dragon parted the skies. Huge fireballs shot from its mouth. Underneath, the very land itself rose up beneath it, twisting and buckling. Witches on brooms turned and fled, those on the ground ran screaming from the plain for the cover of the woodland, Bindnaps and Crooked Hats breathlessly huddled together as the huge beast landed in the ruptured plain, the ground now glowing an ominous bright red, scorching nearby branches.

"What do we do?" someone screamed.

"Hush!" Alfloria commanded, making out a small, familiar figure dismounting from the back of the dragon's neck. "Sinchkin."

In the open, Sinchkin called into the woodland. "Sisters, I am Sinchkin, Grand Tzorkly High Priestess of *The League of Lid-Curving Witchery*." She sent a screaming vroosher into the treetops, pleasantly surprised at how powerful her small wand had become. "I give you all two choices: stay here and stroff yourselves, or come with me."

No one in the woods dare move. Everyone simply watched and waited.

Eventually, a lone twizzled voice called out. "The majicked ground will stroff us, or your sazpent surely will. Either way, we die."

Sinchkin folded her small arms across her chest. "Perhaps not. Perhaps you will be the first one who will have the courage to try." She watched as gradually a dishevelled Bindnapp emerged from the treeline, hesitating at the edge of the glowing ground. "Walk to me with a new allegiance in your heart and no harm will befall you."

The Bindnapp took a tentative step, then another, and another, before suddenly breaking into a run, overwhelming relief writ large on her battle-scarred face.

"You see?" Sinchkin told her. "You simply had to believe."

Others began to follow, slowly emerging from the woodland and running towards her. Some stopped and danced on the glowing red, unable to believe they had been saved from the fire, slapping their hands and whooping as the crowd around Sinchkin and the dragon gradually grew.

Eventually, just one final witch remained. Sinchkin took a deep breath, calling out into the trees. "Alfloria, it seems your armies and plans have deserted you. Now it's time for you to join us."

An angry vroosher shot from the trees by way of reply.

"No harm will come to you. You will be dealt with according to the League's ruling."

The reply echoed over the plain. "Come fight me here. Just you, alone. For I would rather stroff than ever serve the likes of you!"

Sinchkin turned, looked into the enormous sea of expectant faces: Lid Sisters, Bindnapps, Earth Weavers and Crooked Hats, all waiting. "Stay here. No one move."

They watched as the small witch slowly made her way to the trees, wand drawn. Behind, the great dragon raised itself, eyes keenly fixed on the treeline.

At the edge, Sinchkin stopped and peered into the gloom. A sudden blue flash lit the interior and she instinctively ducked, before racing into the woods and seeing an elderly witch dressed in rags bending over Alforia's stroffed body, wand still frizzing. "Who are you?" she asked, wand levelled.

The witch looked up. "Utharde," she quietly replied. "I am a solitary, and have waited many, many moon-turns for this."

"Put away your wand," Sinchkin commanded, nudging Alfloria's body with her foot, aware that other similar witches were now also making their way slowly out of the dense woodland. Some were young, some very old and bent double, but all were dressed in the same rags and battered hats as the elderly assassin.

"There are others, too," Utharde said. "Those who have been hunted and persecuted for too long. Those who are forced to live a life in the shadows, forage for the most splurked scraps and only move under the darkest skies. These are but a fraction of their number, but they will tell others, who tell more still that now they can walk out into the light with a new hope in their hearts."

Sinchkin looked at the sea of sorry faces. Most had terrible scars, missing clumps of fur and rotting teeth. Yet in all their eyes was a silent dignity she'd never seen in any witch before. "You're all," she swallowed, "solitary witches?"

Utharde nodded. "Ready to be respected, accepted and recognised as our own kind."

Sinchkin looked out onto the plain where the others waited.

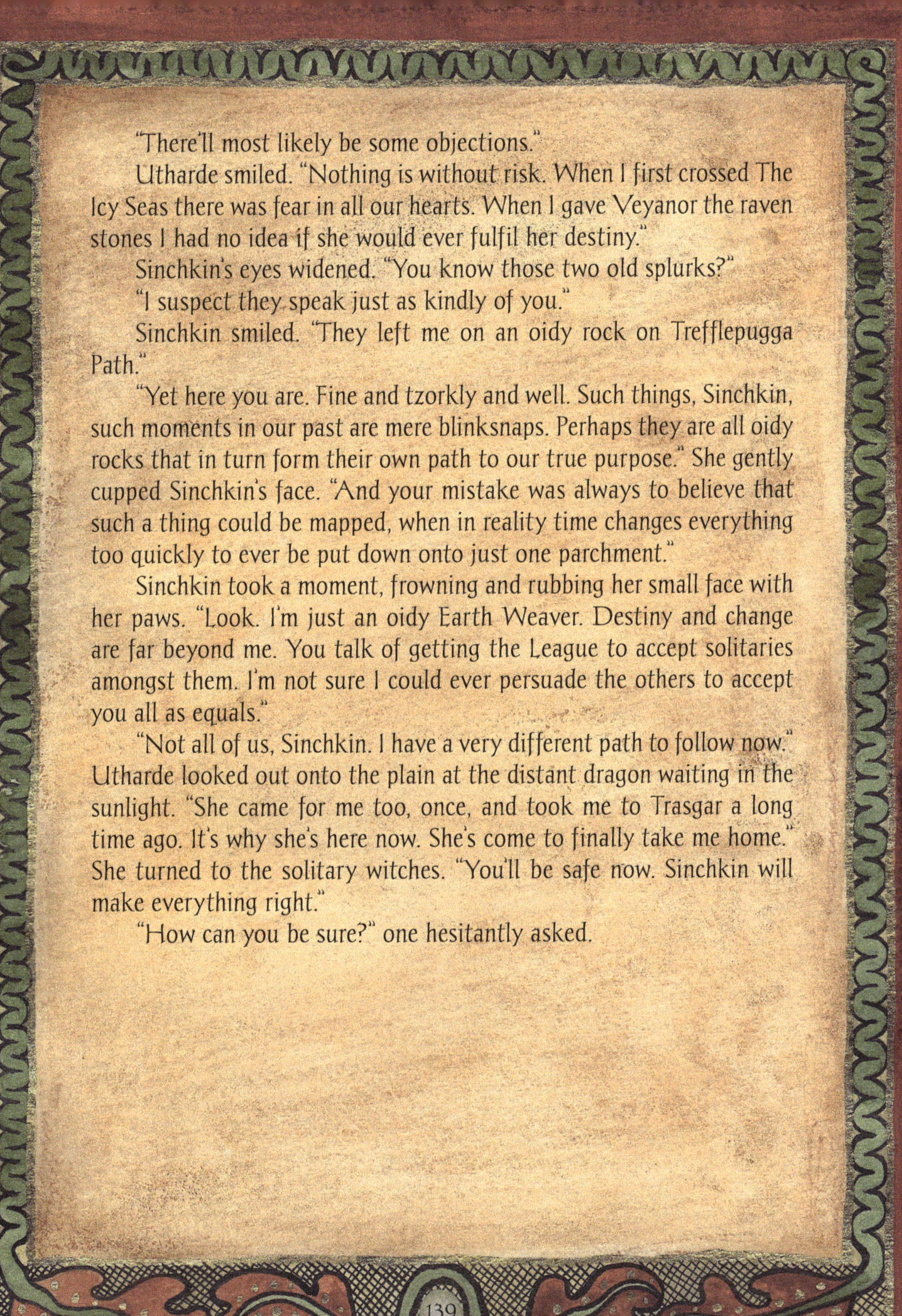

"There'll most likely be some objections."

Utharde smiled. "Nothing is without risk. When I first crossed The Icy Seas there was fear in all our hearts. When I gave Veyanor the raven stones I had no idea if she would ever fulfil her destiny."

Sinchkin's eyes widened. "You know those two old splurks?"

"I suspect they speak just as kindly of you."

Sinchkin smiled. "They left me on an oidy rock on Trefflepugga Path."

"Yet here you are. Fine and tzorkly and well. Such things, Sinchkin, such moments in our past are mere blinksnaps. Perhaps they are all oidy rocks that in turn form their own path to our true purpose." She gently cupped Sinchkin's face. "And your mistake was always to believe that such a thing could be mapped, when in reality time changes everything too quickly to ever be put down onto just one parchment."

Sinchkin took a moment, frowning and rubbing her small face with her paws. "Look. I'm just an oidy Earth Weaver. Destiny and change are far beyond me. You talk of getting the League to accept solitaries amongst them. I'm not sure I could ever persuade the others to accept you all as equals."

"Not all of us, Sinchkin. I have a very different path to follow now." Utharde looked out onto the plain at the distant dragon waiting in the sunlight. "She came for me too, once, and took me to Trasgar a long time ago. It's why she's here now. She's come to finally take me home." She turned to the solitary witches. "You'll be safe now. Sinchkin will make everything right."

"How can you be sure?" one hesitantly asked.

"Because," Utharde quietly replied, "I read it all in some stones, many, many moon-turns ago."

Sinchkin and the others followed Utharde out of the woods and across the plain to where the dragon lay. On seeing her, it let out a great roar, rising on its hind legs and flapping both wings.

She turned to Sinchkin. "Some get to pass to the Ancients in Idla's wings," she smiled. "But I've always wanted a dragon."

The large crowd parted, watching the great beast gently lower his neck for Utharde to climb on. Sinchkin helped as best she could, patting the thick scaly skin. "I won't see you again, then?"

"Not for a long time. You won't need to." She pointed first to Sinchkin's heart, then head. "You have much listening to do, and too much that needs to be done."

Sinchkin tried her best to smile, feeling suddenly too small and quite alone. She cleared her throat. "When I go, I don't want either a dragon or a splurked bird."

Utharde's raised her eyebrows. "Oh, I wouldn't worry. I've already seen what takes you." She winked. "Some of the other Ancients will be quite jealous, I can assure you."

The dragon began to move, Sinchkin and the crowd backing away as it bowed one final time before flapping its huge wings and taking to the air. In its diminishing shadow, Trefflepugga Path also snaked away, the churned ground repairing itself as both disappeared over the distant mountains.

"Well," Sinchkin said, taking a breath and turning to the crowd, "It seems I have a league to build."

Sinchkin's reign as Grand Tzorkly High Priestess of *The League of Lid-Curving Witchery* will be remembered for far more events than can ever be chronicled in just one book. In her time, she achieved many saztaculous, tzorkly and majickal things, managing to unify all four covens and solitary-witches into just one league which grew to number over twenty-thousand strong at the time of her passing.

Indeed, the little Earth Weaver who had bought peace in Dragon's Plain never forgot to rule with both head and heart, but also managed to stay true to her own sense of inquisitiveness and urge for exploration. She herself chronicled many of her own adventures, leaving behind vast rooms of maps, notebooks and sketches, all inscribed with her own system of marks, scribbles and symbols that would one day form the beginnings of the league's Tzorkly Charter that is still honoured and poured over by both dales-creatures and witch-scholars as a unique record of the lifetime of this extraordinary little witch.

When the time came for her to pass to the Ancients, those assembled in her bedchamber remember two things: firstly, that she smiled – and secondly that her last words were, 'Thank goodness it's not the dragon or that splurked bird.' How she travelled on her very final adventure, we'll never know.

In the centuries that followed, much changed in *The League of Lid-Curving Witchery*'s homelands with the arrival of a brand new creature that was to challenge the destiny of this most majickal and tzorkly place forever.

The age of the majickal-hares was about to begin...